Does She Dare?

I should like to acknowledge Iris Dove's pamphlet 'Yours In The Cause – Suffragettes in Lewisham, Greenwich and Woolwich' (1988) which helped me with my research.

B.A.

For more information on books by Bernard Ashley, visit his website

www.bashley.com

Does She Dare?

BERNARD ASHLEY

troika

Published by TROIKA
First published 2017

Troika Books Ltd
Well House, Green Lane, Ardleigh CO7 7PD, UK
www.troikabooks.com

A CIP catalogue record for this book is available
from the British Library

ISBN 978-1-909991-59-0

1 2 3 4 5 6 7 8 9 10

Printed in Poland

The few who dare, must speak and speak again
To right the wrongs of many.

Ella Wheeler Wilcox

Chapter One

Lizzie turned to face the wall and pulled the counterpane over her head. She didn't want to hear the silence from the kitchen. Her father had been shouting at her mother and she knew what was happening now. He was doing something to her in the scullery, and she was stifling her cries so next door wouldn't hear – and nor would she, up here in bed. When the quietness stopped and he said something it would be over for tonight. She burrowed under her pillow and counted to a hundred, but too quickly, because when she came out it was still all quiet down there.

What he was doing could be quick or it could go on, and it could be caused by anything – a button coming off his shirt that morning, his sandwiches too dry, not enough paper on the nail outside in the privy. And from the minute he walked in from work her mother seemed to know what was coming, after which she didn't seem to hear questions the first time and had the look on her face of someone who wasn't really there. He'd be quiet, staring at her in a way that said she was going to cop it when they were on their own.

'Get that homework finished properly, young lady, then get yourself to bed.' Lizzie would try to last it out but he could always wait. Not that what happened was regular, a couple of weeks would go by when there was nothing, other times one bad night would follow another. Who knew when a mistake would get him in a spiteful mood – or when the same annoyance would lead to nothing?

There was never anything to show. Whatever he did he left her mother's face alone so no one in the street could tell. Up here in her bed Lizzie would lie still and imagine how he was hurting her; she'd pinch and twist her own arms, punch her stomach, kick at her ankles and try to hurt herself where she wasn't supposed to touch, but she knew nothing could be as bad as what he was doing downstairs.

Lizzie Ellen Parsons, nearly seventeen and doing well enough at Greenfield Girls' High School not to have been asked to leave; a scholarship scholar from The Slade Elementary School, Plumstead, clean and respectable every day in her green uniform and supposed to think herself lucky. But how lucky was she, lying on a secret like this? And how lucky was her poor mother?

And how respectable was her father, for all his supervisor's job and his bravery medal?

She put her head out again and there was talking down there. Not by her mother, she'd be dabbing herself with a cloth in the scullery, with a pink calamine lotion tinge to it the next day – it would be him, going on about something at work, moaning like anyone normal as if he'd done nothing to her just now. Those nights there was a monotony about his voice; you didn't have to hear the words to tell the difference between his usual grousing and times like this. And in the mornings he'd be a Royal Arsenal supervisor again, off to work at the ordnance factory. And her mother would be quiet, concentrating on the breakfast and the sandwiches. But after that first time when a muffled cry had carried upstairs, the pink cloth at the sink and the rolled-down sleeves next morning had given everything away. All three of them had their privacy when the bath was brought in, and at the kitchen sink for their morning wash, so Lizzie had never seen what he did to her – but it was something horrible, she knew that for certain.

So why didn't her mother say anything? There were uncles somewhere who could stand up for her, surely? Lizzie turned herself over and tightened up in a ball. Or why didn't *she* say something? If not to someone else, to her mother, let her know that she knew something bad was going on? Shouldn't she help her to stand up to him? That question was never out of her head, and after a bad night it always got stronger as she walked towards the house after school next day.

And Lizzie knew the answer to it. Her mother didn't want her to know or she'd say something, or she'd cry out loudly when it happened, shout and scream till Lizzie ran downstairs. Alice Parsons was a proud woman and she was taking what he dished out to keep the three of them together, but wasn't that too easy an excuse for saying nothing herself? The hard, truthful answer was she was scared of her father. He'd never laid a finger on her, although little Freddie had taken a clout or two before he'd died of scarlet fever. No, she was scared of what he'd do to her if she ran downstairs and shouted at him to stop. So on those bad nights she stewed in bed instead.

She had thought about saying something to Miss Mitchell. Miss Mitchell taught history, and wasn't as old as most of the other teachers. You could talk to her, and she often spoke to the form about things going on in the world, like how there might be a war, and what women could do if there were. But what could Miss Mitchell do about the father of a girl whose mother was being treated badly? Eliza Parsons wouldn't be the only girl in the school with a problem like that, any more than she'd be the only girl along Sutcliffe Road.

So like most nights she eventually got off to sleep;

next morning would be another day, and in with the daylight would come the happier thought that she might see Joe Gibson again. And that was a prospect to give her a lift.

She first met Joe at school, which was weird because Greenfield High was a girls' school, and weird, too, because it was at the top of Shooters Hill and he lived quite near, but she'd never seen him before. He had pulled a handcart of paraffin and candles up to the school and it must have been his first time there because when he came into the vestibule he went very red and looked as if he'd walked into a dream: all these girls at lesson change. And then he dropped a can and the paraffin ran gleaming over the floor and into the cracks and grooves. But she didn't laugh like the others – he looked so devastated. His arms and legs went four different ways trying to stop the roll of the can before it emptied itself out with a gurgle. She helped by quickly scooping it up, and then making him take his boots off before he trod paraffin over everywhere.

Ruffage the janitor came running with a bucket of water and a mop. 'Stop!' He put his palm up to a line of first formers coming down the stairs. 'Light no matches!' There was a great bustle which made everyone late for the next lesson, but Lizzie was allowed to stay and help – more with the boy's boots than the floor – and after his ears had been pinned back by the deputy headmistress for coming in by the front door he retreated to his cart outside, leaving his cap behind. Which Lizzie took out to him.

With the front door shut he shrugged and smiled. 'Thought I'd ginger things up a bit.'

'You did that all right. It'll pong for weeks.'

'I won't get to come here again. She'll tell Smollett.' Even standing still he was awkward, as if he might flap his arms any second and fly off; tall, with a darned jumper and haywire hair.

'I don't suppose you will.'

'More's the pity.' He looked her in the eyes and with a little bow he took his cap from her and put it on, jaunty-style.

She turned to go back inside. Miss Gale would know to the second how long it should take to give back a cap.

'I think I've seen you before.' He squinted at her with one eye half closed. 'Yes. Last Christmas, the carols. Your people from the Mission were at the Ascension Hall. You sang the part of Mary in a sketch.'

'In a scene.' She remembered baby Jesus' chipped china face, but she didn't remember him.

'I was at the organ.'

'Really?' He had played it very well.

'Pumping it from behind.' He stood looking at her.

'So we're both a bit musical, aren't we?'

'I suppose we are.'

'Eliza!' Miss Gale was at the top of the steps. 'Come inside now, please.'

'Yes, madam.' Lizzie turned to go in.

'Eliza, eh?' He gave her a little bow. 'I'm Joseph. Joe Gibson.'

'I'm Lizzie. Lizzie Parsons.' She went inside, but as she snatched up her books from the hall table she heard something else: a whistling from the road, quite loud and with a flourish to it: the song her mother sometimes sang, 'Let Me Call You Sweetheart'. And that sent her to history with a smile on her face.

Joe Gibson was the youngest of three boys – by a long chalk. The other two had been in the Royal Artillery for some time and lived their own regimental lives, leaving Joe with their grandmother, Emma. When either of them came home on leave they called her 'Emma-Sarah-Demerara-Semolina-Tapioca' and joshed her for being on the short side – picked her up and sat her on a table, gave her a piggyback around the garden, or sat on top of her in an armchair as if she weren't there. And they joshed Joe, too, for being tall and gangly and having two left feet. 'You could no more be a soldier than Emma-Sarah . . .' And then she'd chase them with a broom.

'I could still give you a walloping you wouldn't forget!'

On their own, Gran and Joe rubbed along nicely. His mother had died giving birth to a stillborn sister when he was two, and his father had gone off with the army to India, the last anyone ever heard of him. So Gran had been a mother to Joe. And the day after he left school he was marched into Smollett's Stores on Woolwich Common Road.

'Mr Smollett.' She knew Smollett, and he looked at her with a wary eye. 'You'll be pleased to know my grandson Joseph has left Wickham Lane Boys' and he's looking for a job.'

The pleasure seemed to elude Smollett. He stared at Joe through a frown, puffed out his cheeks. 'Just left school?' He looked him up and down, twice.

'He's tall for his age. Could easy reach high places.' Gran Gibson nodded at the window pole used for nudging items off top shelves.

Smollett pinched his nose and waggled it. He flapped a fat hand at a public health certificate framed on the wall. 'Has the boy got any qualifications, Mrs Gibson? Apart from having a fair stretch?'

'No, he never took up any space on the honours board. But he's got a good honest pair of hands and a good heart, and I straight-off thought of you to have him.' She put her head on one side like a robin.

Smollett lifted a batch of invoices off a spike and put them back again, played left-hand piano on the counter. 'You hadn't thought of the Royal Arsenal down the road, in the ammunition shops? I hear they're taking people on. There's trouble brewing Turkey way, and money to be made out of war . . .' He rubbed his fat fingers. 'Fish to fry.'

'And a stinking business, too, guns and bullets. No, he needs a clean, responsible job where he can use his brain, because he's got a good one, even if it doesn't always reach to the end of a pencil.'

Smollett looked at Joe, cap in hand, Sunday jacket, best boots, hair more or less tamed for the time being. He fixed him with another waggle of the nose. 'Well, tell me this, boy: if I were to give you a two-pound cheese and told you to cut six ounces off it, what would I be left with?'

Joe answered before the man could lace his fingers. 'One pound, ten ounces, sir.'

'Eh?' Smollett seemed surprised at the speed of Joe's answer. 'Very good.' He stared at the ceiling. 'Now then. A customer's got a pound note in his pocket and spends twelve shillings and threepence-three-farthings. How much change do you give him?' He nodded smugly.

Joe scratched his cheek briefly. 'Er . . . seven an' eight-pence farthing, sir.'

Gran Gibson was folding her arms at Smollett.

'Blow me down!' The man suddenly became decisive. 'Start Monday morning, seven o'clock in a clean collar.'

'Yes, sir. Thank you very much, sir.'

'Thank you, Mr Smollett.' Gran smoothed the wrinkles out of her gloves, left and right. 'We can talk about remuneration when you've had a little think.'

'I shall ponder. They were certainly snappy answers the boy gave me.'

'I told you he's quick.' She smiled, took Joe by his coat sleeve and led him out of the shop.

Joe walked away from the doorway and stopped. 'How did you know Smollett was going to ask those very questions?'

'*Mr* Smollett to you.' She walked on. 'Because I used to work for him, and he always asked the same sums, taking on a boy. Got no imagination, for all his money.' And she pursed up her lips in a victorious way, like beating Joe at cards. 'But you watch your p's and q's, Joseph Gibson because he's no fool, old Smollett.'

Lizzie came out of school with her friend Flo, hugging as they said goodbye to go their different ways. At the end of lessons Lizzie had brushed her hair, set her beret at a slight angle, and smoothed down her uniform dress. But of course Joe wouldn't be outside; he worked at Smollett's and the shop didn't shut till late.

She headed towards home and that familiar dread started twisting her insides. Her father would still be at work but her mother would be in, so she and Mum would be alone together, and she *had* to say something today. She couldn't imagine any of her schoolmistresses keeping quiet about being treated like her mother. They were women who could stand up for themselves, they would take action, tell their pastor or a Justice of the Peace, say something to another relative – so why couldn't her mother? She had got to be persuaded to at least tell an aunt or uncle what was going on.

Lizzie felt all mixed-up about her father. He was always very straight with her, although kind enough; not a cuddly man but not a cold one, either, and he'd been so proud of her winning the Greenfield scholarship that he'd made her wear her uniform home from the outfitters, never mind that she didn't start for half a term. He never said anything about her mother's letter-writing for neighbours, but he would come to the table to look over any school homework being done, and, 'Very neat writing, very neat,' he'd say and sit down again with a grunt as if he'd marked it. He never smacked her, but then he rarely kissed her, either – a peck on the forehead and a hand on the shoulder was his way of saying goodnight. He'd never read her a story nor put her to bed; there'd been no romps, and even when he was holding her by the arm he was like a coal man with a vase. But the sound of him laughing or pulling out a twist of sherbert could always get her smiling.

So was she a traitor to her mother if she still loved him?

She turned into her street, beginning to feel breathless with what she'd got to say as soon as she got indoors – because if she didn't say it quickly she knew she wouldn't say it at all.

She knocked and her mother called, 'Coming!' in a cheerful voice – and when the door was opened she gave her a big, loving smile. 'Lizzie, lamb!'

'Hello, Mum.'

'My word, you look hot.'

'It's a bit of a swelterer.' Which it wasn't. This was *her.*

'Have a glass of cold water.'

Lizzie followed her through to the scullery. The houses in Sutcliffe Road were two-up and two-down with back additions. She gulped down a glass of water as her mother leant across the sink and pulled the lace curtain aside.

'Now, just admire that line-full of washing!' Lizzie saw the sheets and pillowcases flapping idly on the line. 'My whites beat all around, don't you think?' Her mother said it with pride and with pleasure. 'It's the blue-bag does it.'

'It certainly does.' *And with no pink marks on them.* Now was the moment. She drew in a shallow breath – but her mother had started singing.

'Rejoice the Lord is King!
Your Lord and King adore;
mortals give thanks and sing,
and triumph evermore.
lift up your heart,
lift up your voice;
rejoice again I say, rejoice.'

Her face was rosy with the work of washday, and she gave a confidential wink as she pulled the blotting paper over her letter-writing on the table, something for a neighbour. She began to put her pen and her papers into her writing box. 'I'll clear some space and you can get on with your homework.

'Jesus the Saviour reigns,
the God of truth and love . . .'

'No, that's all right.' Lizzie knew her mother was good at keeping neighbours' secrets – as well as hiding her own. 'I've got something I want to say to you . . .' Lizzie turned to look along the hallway, her back to the kitchen, meaning she didn't have to face her mother. She drew in another shaky breath.

'I love that hymn, Lizzie, the words and the tune are like songbirds in the sky. I've copied the music for the Mission organ, easier for Miss Rush to see.' She sounded very satisfied with what she'd done.

'Now, listen, Mum –'

'Lift up your heart,

Lift up your voice . . .

'I'm all ears. Come on, lamb, what is it you want to say?' She seemed so untroubled and happy.

'Well . . .' Lizzie turned back again to see a calm, smiling face. Truly, her mother was nothing like she'd been last night; she didn't look as if she'd been crying, she hadn't been too shaky to do her letter-writing nor too weak to do that big wash. She was so calm and content – and happy-looking. Lizzie opened her mouth and closed it. Getting all wound up to say something had put doubt in her mind – and she had to be very, very sure she wasn't making a terrible mistake. What if she'd been completely wrong and the things she'd imagined were just not true?

Her resolution had gone. She pulled up a chair at the kitchen table, put the stopper in her mother's inkpot, and sat with her hands palm down on the cloth like someone about to open a meeting. She lifted her chin. 'It's just, I've got a bit of good news to tell you.'

'Bravo!' Her mother beamed, already sharing in it. 'Lizzie, what can it be?'

Lizzie smiled back at her and folded her arms. 'Well, sit down, Mum, and I'll tell you.'

Chapter Two

'I'm sitting down. Go on!' Her mother's face was all expectation.

Lizzie came straight out with it. 'Miss Abrahams kept me behind after the English lesson this morning.'

'That doesn't sound good news.'

Lizzie smiled. 'She said she's having a quiet word with a few other girls to see if they want to do it.'

'Fill up the inkwells? That's what I used to be saddled with.'

'No, something more special than that. To go in for this poetry competition . . .'

'Mount Vesuvius! My poetess! Is this a school competition?'

Lizzie lifted her head higher than it had been all day. 'National!'

'A *national* competition?'

'All over the country. You know how the school

isn't just on its own, it belongs to a big . . .' She couldn't find the word, made a globe with her hands.

'League. The League of British Girls' Schools . . .'

'Yes, them. Well, they have a big meeting once a year at the Westminster Central Hall, and this year every Trust school can enter a poem written by a girl. And the winner out of all the schools recites it from the platform on the day . . .'

'Heavens! What an honour, Lizzie, what an honour!'

'Miss Abrahams said there are more than thirty schools; each school can enter one poem, and a panel of judges picks the best one to be recited. She says it's a huge fillip for the winning school.'

'I should think so, too.' Her mother sat back and opened her arms. 'Well, well, well! My girl! Miss Abrahams asked *you*!' She dropped her voice, and nodded. 'She knows you could do Greenfield proud . . .' And the look on her face told Lizzie she had done the right thing, changing her mind about what to say. For now. Just for today. And at this proud moment she knew that if she wrote a poem called 'Happiness' it would be all about her mother's bright eyes and smiling mouth right then. Because it *was* something to be asked. Miss Abrahams never did anything lightly, from opening a book to awarding a merit mark, so she had to think Eliza Parsons had a fair chance among the others.

There was a slight angle to her mother's head. 'Of

course, we mustn't get ahead of ourselves – but just to be asked by Miss Abrahams is a great privilege . . . Is she the tall one?'

'That's Miss Mitchell.' Miss Mitchell was tall, and beautiful. Miss Abrahams was short and older and wore noisy shoes.

'To be selected to *try* – a Plumstead scholarship pupil, amongst all those Eltham and Blackheath girls. Has the League decided on a title? For the poem? Can you write whatever you want, or does it have to be on a particular subject – like, Beauty, or Daffodils, or a Grecian Urn?'

'She says it must be something we feel strongly about.' Although, as she said it, Lizzie wondered what she *did* feel strongly about. There were lots of things she felt keen on, that she cared about, like horses being whipped up Shooters Hill, but *strongly*? She could think of girls at Greenfield who went on about things as if they were life or death important, girls whose fathers were doctors or generals or judges, while she was just Lizzie Parsons, no one special. And with all their clever brains it probably wouldn't be her ending up as the Poet of the Central Hall, would it?

But the news – and the way her mother had been this afternoon – had certainly put a different glow into the sky.

'Just wait till your father comes in. Won't he be

pleased?' Which took only a little of that glow away.

Jack Parsons was a respected man. Walking in and out through the gate of the Woolwich Arsenal he was never searched by the police – a cartridge shop supervisor would never be so stupid as to carry tobacco and matches into a munitions factory.

The eight-to-six shift in Small Arms Factory Number Three had begun on the hooter that morning, when he'd stood ready at the cartridge shop door; tall, his oiled hair centrally parted and his face shaven shiny-close. With his watch in his hand he had seen the cartridge fillers in, and now, after the day's work was done, he took his watch from his pocket to open the shop door and see them out. He wasn't allowed to search the men except with his eyes, but he would stare into every face, and that was enough to keep them from the temptation of stealing brass for scrap. Few would want to go against Jack Parsons, anyway, and whenever he rolled up his sleeves, the reason for their respect could be seen. Yes, he was a shop supervisor with a down on the Union, but the ugly scars on his arms were evidence of the day he'd dragged a trolley of exploding rockets clear of the Signals Depot and saved thirty members' lives – a deed for which he'd been awarded the Edward Medal for bravery.

Most men gave him a polite nod as they went out,

but Fred Mason never did; a strong Union man, he rarely had a word for this supervisor, either coming in or going out.

'You were three minutes late this morning, Mason. Did you take it out of your dinner break?'

'You know I did. Your watch was in and out of your pocket like it was on elastic. But you can bet your backside I'll give the driver of my number forty-two a few choice words for letting a horse drop dead across his tramlines.' He pulled his cap hard down on his head and went out.

Jack Parsons didn't smile. But he found one for the female cleaner coming in. 'Evening, Dolly.'

'Evening, Jack.' She was younger than him, pretty, wore her work cap with a saucy tilt and showed more curls than she should. She lingered while the last of the men went out. 'Got anything nice for your tea tonight?'

'Being Monday, probably a slice of cold pork.'

'Poor old Jack. I've got something hot.' She gave him a wink and went inside with her broom.

He buttoned his jacket slowly and walked through to the gate, to head up the hill to Sutcliffe Road – where it turned out that he'd been right: it was cold pork for tea. Lizzie took sandwiches to school, and because Jack did, too, Alice always made tea into a dinner sort of meal, and tonight it was yesterday's pork dished up cold with hot gravy.

He hung his cap in the hall and went into the kitchen, stood and looked at the table. 'Not laid up yet?'

'Won't take long, Jack. We've been sharing good news, Lizzie and me.' Alice cleared away her pen and paper.

'Good news, eh? Well, what could that be?'

Lizzie was on her feet, her face flushed. She smiled at her father, who was folding his arms in a 'well-isn't-this-nice?' sort of way, waiting to be pleased. She gabbled out her news, knowing that what she did at Greenfield High meant the world to him; he'd be telling this to everyone he knew. She made a lot of the League of British Girls' Schools side of things, and the words 'Westminster Central Hall' had never been pronounced with so much plum.

He put his hands on her shoulders, gripped and squeezed them in a little rhythm, as if his fingers were saying something. 'You're doing yourself proud, Eliza Parsons, you're a credit to me; and to your mother.'

'Isn't that good news, Jack?'

'It is. It is.' He took off his jacket, threw it over the back of his easy chair, and sat. 'A poem, eh? For the Westminster Central Hall. Well, I'll have to give you a leg-up with that, won't I?' He closed his eyes. 'Now, let me think . . .'

Lizzie stayed waiting. Her father could be a difficult man, and her suspicions over those bad nights had made her very unsure of him; but look at how happy her mother had been today, and at how kind he was being right now.

He cleared his throat. 'Of course, I'm no Robert Wordsworth, but how about . . .' He put on a musing face.

'I like the smell of an English rose,

I like the look . . . of swallers in the sky.

. . . But most of all . . . if you're pleasing me

I like the taste of a hot meat pie.'

He laughed like gunshots, and Lizzie and her mother joined in.

'Tea won't be long.' Alice went to the scullery, while Lizzie laid the table.

'In the meantime a cuppa for a dry-as-dust working man would be welcome.' He went on smiling to himself while Lizzie scooted to get him one. She didn't want anything to change his mood.

At bedtime she was able to go up the stairs content. The meal was over, and as a treat she'd been let into the parlour to sit and do her homework; being summer it didn't need a fire. And she somehow felt sure that tonight she wouldn't be lying awake listening for ominous sounds from below.

But she still couldn't get off to sleep. Downstairs the voices were normal, her mother doing most of the talking, so it wasn't recent fears that kept her awake;

but with her world feeling more settled, it was Joe Gibson. And last Saturday night.

Joe Gibson.

She curled herself up. He was a funny boy, and she'd met lots of funny boys – from little children at school through to dandy lads around Plumstead – but she'd never met anyone like Joe Gibson. He could be funny, but underneath there was something serious about him with his quiet, deep voice that seemed to give extra meaning to his words.

This had been at the Plumstead Hall on Saturday evening when she'd gone with a group from the Mission young people's club. A cinematograph film of *Oliver Twist* was being shown, over an hour long, and in one of the reel changes who did she see in the vestibule but the boy who'd spilt paraffin at Greenfield High? He did a little bow like the Artful Dodger, and she lifted her chin like Nancy.

'Hello.'

'Hello, Lizzie.'

'What are you doing here?'

He stood to attention and looked important. 'I came in case the cinematograph breaks down, or the lamp goes bang.'

'Really?'

'I'm standing by to act all the parts: Oliver Twist, Fagin, Nancy . . .' said with a little curtsey. 'Except I don't know the end of the story, so I'll have to make it up. I think Fagin jumps off London Bridge and drowns. I can do a good drowning . . .' He floundered his arms about, going under.

She put her hands on her hips. 'Sounds to me like you're good at making things up.'

'And I think you're right.' He stood still with only the slightest wobble. 'No, I came with our church lads . . .'

'From the Ascension?'

'You remembered.'

'Well, I couldn't forget a boy who's changed the smell of Greenfield High School for a few weeks, could I?'

He bowed again as if he'd done the school a favour, but he was caught in the act by the call to go back for the next reel of film. And as they walked into the hall he asked her, 'Do you know The Slade Pond?'

'Of course I do. I could almost throw a stone in it from our front garden.'

'Well, how about I see you there Sunday afternoon, about four o'clock? Not tomorrow – the Sunday after?'

What? That made her catch her breath. 'Oh, I don't know. I might.' On Sundays at three o'clock she taught a class at the Mission Sunday school, then it was usually a walk with her friends until teatime. Now she was being asked to meet this boy instead. She wanted to smile but she kept a steady stare. 'I'll have to see.'

'Well, I'll be there, anyway. I'll be waiting.'

She nodded, and went back to her seat to see Bill Sikes murdering Nancy – which the man at the cinematograph took at a lick, cranking fast towards a happy ending for Oliver.

But somehow Lizzie wasn't concentrating very hard any more. And by the look on his face in the light of the lamp, neither was Joe Gibson.

Lizzie made the meeting on the Sunday. While changing after dinner she checked herself in the swivel mirror on her dressing table, just to see whom Joe would be meeting that afternoon: a prettyish girl with hazel eyes and dark hair that wasn't a crowning glory, so cut shortish and straight by Mrs Sprey on The Slade. With an angling of the mirror and a step back she saw someone standing tall and slim with a pair of hands that looked good in Sunday gloves. She stepped towards the mirror again and flashed her eyes at herself, quite out of character for a Sunday school teacher. She ran downstairs and called her goodbyes into the kitchen, stepping out into the street. Being one of the older girls at the Mission she told Bible stories to a group of six-year-olds. This week it was 'The Loaves and the Fishes' – and like the film projectionist with *Oliver Twist* she got through it at a fair pace so her class could be ready to go home on the dot. Now, dressed in her summer coat and beret she came out of the Mission Hall making excuses to her friends for having something to do for her mother. But instead of turning into Sutcliffe Road, she went down the steps towards the large pond at the bottom of The Slade Ravine – her meeting place with Joe.

So was her stomach turning over because he might not come, or the thought that he would? Their two meetings so far had been by chance, but this was different, it was something arranged. The ravine was said to be an ice-age valley, but right now she felt warm in her summer clothes. The steps led her down past thick gorse bushes to the northern end of the ravine and to a seat where anyone meeting at the pond would go. But the seat was empty – he'd said he'd be waiting – and a sudden sour smell seemed to come off the water. A muddy path went around the pond but there was no one on it, no sign of life except the overhanging trees and the flap of a duck trying to fly, certainly no sign of the boy whose face she couldn't see in her head any more.

There was no Joe Gibson at The Slade Pond.

She didn't know quite what time it was, it had to be about a quarter past four – and he'd said four o'clock. So was he a chancer? Did he fix up meetings with different girls and picked the one he fancied most?

Had he met someone else on the Sunday in between and was walking her out instead? All day she'd been thinking about this meeting, and Miss Rush at the Mission had remarked on her pretty smile. Now the ravine had turned chilly, and she didn't like this gripe inside of not knowing how things would end up.

She turned to face the steps again. What was she to do – go for a walk on her own and get indoors at around the usual time? She looked all about her, but there was still no one to be seen, and the dark side of her brain asked if this was what life was all about – a build-up and then a big let-down? Well, she told herself, one of her father's sayings was right: you lived and learned, you lived and learned. And so was another. 'If you don't let your hopes fly too high, you won't get hurt when they come crashing down.' Which was a pity, because she'd thought better of Joe Gibson, going by the couple of times she'd met him. Quite a bit better.

Chapter Three

Joe Gibson stood dressed in his best jacket, clean collar and cuffs, his hair flattened with water. He and Gran had been to church, he'd pumped the organ for sixpence and put the money in the Waifs and Strays box, then come home for his Sunday dinner. He'd helped to wash up and now Gran was about to sit in her chair for her Sunday afternoon nap.

'You want to be careful where you go when you're out.' Her voice was flat and serious.

'Why's that?'

'If you have to take off your cap that hair's going to spring up like Shock-headed Peter . . .'

He licked his palms and smarmed it down again.

'Or put the wind up whoever you're all dressed-up for . . .'

He gave her a cool look.

'. . . Not that I want to know who it is.'

'Course you don't!'

This was how they lived, with banter and love – in a small cottage at the country end of Garland Road.

'Just remember your p's an' q's. Use your handkerchief, not your sleeve – an' walk on the outside of the pavement if you're with a young lady.'

'You're fishing, aren't you?'

'Oh? And what would I be fishing for?'

'Where I'm going. What I'm up to.' He took his best cap off its hook and went to the front door.

She got up and went with him. 'Only 'cos you're acting so damned secret.' She dusted her hands of him. 'I don't give a fig. But you look dapper enough for going anywhere so don't let yourself down. Be good!' And she aimed a kick at his backside – but he was an inch too quick for her.

Lizzie was halfway up the ravine steps when she heard the whistling. It came from behind her, down by the pond, and after a first pierce like someone summoning, it went into the tune of 'Let me call you sweetheart'. There was no doubt who that was. And, yes, Joe Gibson was standing by the seat waving an arm. The sun came out and put a glint on the water, and Lizzie only just stopped herself from skipping down to him.

'Given up on me, Eliza?'

'Lizzie, if you don't mind! Well, you did say four o'clock . . .'

'I said, "*About* four o'clock."' He looked around him. 'With my gran,' he said in a low voice, 'you can't set your sundial by Sunday dinner time. It's all according to how much she has to stop and think about the vicar's wise words.'

'Ah.' Lizzie's Sunday dinner had to be cooked, eaten, washed up and put away by the tick of her father's watch.

'Besides, I came the long way round, past the cemetery.'

'Oh, dear!'

'No, there's an old flower seller outside.' He put his hand into his jacket and brought out a posy of blue anemones. 'Grecian Windflowers, she calls them.' He offered them to her like a boy on a valentine postcard.

Lizzie took them, surprised. When she was little at school Danny Johnson had given her a snail in exchange for a kiss, but no boy had ever offered her anything since. 'Thank you.' She smelt them – slightly pungent. 'Mmm. They're lovely.'

'They go with your eyes.'

'They're not blue.'

'But they're pretty.'

The cheeky thing! She stared at him but he just put his head on one side; he was a bit of a lad, this Joe.

'Shall we go for a stroll?' He pointed towards the head of the ravine. 'Or do you fancy a paddle?'

'It's too deep, thank you.'

'And who knows what's lurking underneath. Come on.' He led the way along the pond track and up towards Lizzie's old school and the shops.

'Where do you live?' She hadn't seen which way he'd come, except it wasn't down her steps.

'Up there past the school. Top end of Garland Road where the fields start.'

The Slade had been her school, but he hadn't come to it. 'Which school was yours, then?'

'Wickham Lane. We lived near it when I started, and I stayed on when we moved.'

'Ah.' There was a lot more she wanted to know about him but she wasn't going to ask everything at once. 'Are you still spilling paraffin all over the place?'

'No, Smollett won't let me take that sort of stuff out on the handcart; not since your Lady Muck kicked up a shindy . . .'

'Miss Gale? She's quite kind, really. More likely the janitor!'

They came up from the ravine, walking together but with him leading – along past the cricket pitch on the common.

'Nice man, is he? Mr Smollett?'

'Smollett!' Joe scratched his head through his cap.

'Not very.' He stopped and turned to her. '"Fetch me a rub of putty," he said the other day. "Have we got a broken a window out the back?" I ask him. "Just fetch it, an' get that floor swept, after." So I fetch the putty but he just puts it on the counter, not looking at it while I'm there. So I take myself and my broom behind a couple of sacks and I watch him. And what does he do?' Joe leant his head towards her and made slits of his eyes. 'He goes over to the scales and puts a dob of putty under the pan. Not a lot. Just a dob.' Joe folded his arms and Lizzie saw a quick flash of something in his eyes, like the spark from a flint. 'So when a customer reckons they've got half a pound of something, they haven't – they're a pennyweight short.'

Joe had started off funny, imitating Smollett's voice, puffing out the man's words like smoke rings, but now he was serious, his eyes unblinking.

'That's criminal!'

'It's typical of half his sort. Their fiddles and their diddles make money out of anyone who's got no clout. He gives tick till the end of the week, an' you should see the alterations in his book when the customer's gone out of the shop: he puts a farthing on here, a ha'penny there, then he adds it up wrong anyway. Old Mrs Bowyer came in yesterday. Her husband's dead and she rents one of his houses in Barden Street so he's got her where he wants her. She queries his adding-up

– turns out she's got it on a piece of paper, to check. "If you don't trust me, Lil Bowyer," he says, "you can take your custom elsewhere an' drop your door-key on the counter as you go." She pays up of course. "Business is business," he says when she's gone. Then he laughs. "And she's not got some big husband to come and bonk me on the nose."'

His story had started out as talk, now it was a rant. Lizzie had gone quiet, and Joe kicked a foot forward to start walking again. 'Sorry. Don't mind me. I get a bit het up about some sorts of things.'

Just like her dad, Lizzie thought, but in a different way. 'I mustn't be too long now, Joe.'

'I've done it, haven't I?' He stopped again. 'You won't want to come out again, me getting all hot under the collar.'

'Don't be silly. But . . .'

'I'll walk you back.'

'Thank you.' It was a good idea. Thought of her father had put the picture in her head of him walking home from one of his mooches right now.

They took a short cut across the cricket pitch and walked back towards the pond – silent for most of the way. Until, 'Smollett shuts up sharp on a Saturday to get in a couple of after-work pints at the Traders' Club.' He was a bit more of the old Joe now, the boy who'd spilt the paraffin. 'And next Saturday I'm going to see a man-eating lion being let loose on a crowd of Christians in the Plumstead Hall.' His eyes rolled.

'*What?*'

'The cinematograph: *Nero and the Fall of Rome.* Want to come?'

'Oh, I don't know about that . . .'

'Well, think about it, eh?'

'I was allowed to come last time because we're reading *Oliver Twist* at school.'

'Yeah? Well, say you're reading a bit of Roman history.'

'And I'd have to tell them a fib.' She let it go at that and hurried them back to the pond. They stood by the seat.

'I *might* see you on Saturday, then? Seven o'clock?'

'I told you, I'm not sure.' And she truly wasn't.

'I'll say cheerio, then.'

'Yes, cheerio. Thanks for the anemones.' She gave them a little shake.

'That's all right.' He bowed. '*Grecian Windflowers.*' And went, walking off along the pond track, not looking back to wave. She waited until he was out of sight and threw the posy into the pond. Well, she couldn't take them home, could she? They might think she'd robbed them off a grave . . .

The moment she got indoors Lizzie's hopes about her

father withered. Her mother turned her face away but there was crying all over it, blotchy and red.

'Are you all right, Mum?'

'That boiler. I put a match to the gas but I wasn't quick enough. It came out at me like a blow lamp. Put my arm up, but . . .' She was pulling the sleeve of her blouse down over her wrist. 'Can you smell the singe of my hair?'

Lizzie couldn't, and her mother's hair looked all right.

'Dad go out?'

'For his mooch somewhere. Not back yet.'

'Let's have a look.'

'I'm all right. No real damage done.' Her mother pulled away. 'I've left a mess in the kitchen. You take your best things upstairs.'

But Lizzie followed her through, where a dishcloth was thrown over the table. But what was there couldn't be hidden: the Sunday cake wasn't the cake she'd seen in the larder; this was a crumbled mess, as if it had been mangled in somebody's fingers.

'I dropped it, bringing it out. Dad's favourite, Dundee. So he's in a paddy.' They looked at one another, and Lizzie knew that wasn't the truth of things. Something had happened between them after she'd left for Sunday school.

'I'm sorry, Mum.' She picked at the scattered

debris. If she could help put things right perhaps her father's paddy would blow itself away. 'I know what! How about if we mix the crumbs with honey, press them into balls, and push them down into cups. Then we could turn them out on to plates and call them, "Alice Parsons's Disasters".'

But there wasn't a laugh to be had over this, and although they tried to salvage some of the cake it didn't work – and when her father came back, their tea was bread and jam and half an apple with a marshmallow treat brought out, which he pushed aside with the back of his hand.

Lizzie washed up and cleared away, tried to string it out; and she also tried to string out the homework she'd already done, but there was still light in the sky when she was sent to bed – to lie there the way she had before, tight-curled and imagining what was going on in the silence downstairs.

With no room tonight for Joe Gibson in her thoughts.

Monday was a history day, in the last lesson before dinner – meaning that Lizzie could speak to Miss Mitchell without being late for anyone else. Miss Charlotte Mitchell with her long fair hair in a loose net, her blue eyes and her serious smile. Most lessons ended up with girls wanting to speak to her, but Lizzie would hang back today; what she wanted to say to the mistress was very private. But how to start, and how much to tell? This had woken her early. She had no evidence she could show for what was going on at home – those pink calamine lotion cloths weren't the same as pink washed-out-blood cloths – and she knew her mother would act her head off rather than point a finger at her husband.

Lizzie sat taut and tense through the lesson, unable to concentrate on the ins and outs of the Rump Parliament – because the words she wanted to say to Miss Mitchell didn't sound nearly as good this morning as they had the night before. Whichever way she changed them around they were either too sensational or too vague. So she'd just have to hope they came out right when she opened her mouth. But what could be harder than telling a schoolmistress that her father was doing spiteful things to her mother? And what would happen when she did? Would Miss Mitchell keep it to herself, or would she have to tell the headmistress Miss Tudor Hart, and would Miss Tudor Hart – who was a Justice of the Peace – have to tell the police? Then who would they believe: hero Jack Parsons with the bravery medal, or his wife, who could have done things to herself?

There was no clock in the room, the school day was measured by bells, and as the lesson moved nearer and nearer to its end Lizzie's breathing came shorter and she felt light-headed, scared that when the bell rang she'd jump out of her desk, or faint. So she had to try to be calm, and to be brave. She counted to a hundred and did it again. She thought of her mother and the funny monologues she did at Christmas with a twinkle in her eye. She thought of her kindness in reading and writing people's letters without making them feel stupid. She thought how Miss Rush at the Mission Hall could go on playing the organ because Alice Parsons rewrote her music larger; and how there was always a drop of milk for Mrs Farmer next door when the children would otherwise go short. Most of all she thought of how her mother was always by her side with a cuddle or a kiss or a loving word – and always had been. And she wanted to cry when she thought how no one in the world deserved to be harmed, but Alice Parsons deserved it least of all.

These thoughts somehow helped – and when the bell rang she didn't jump or faint but moved out of the desk to go the front.

'Sandwich time!' Flo usually led the way to the lockers.

'There's something I want to ask. I'll see you later.'

'Ask her how long before we get to chopping off King Charles's head.' For a quiet girl with Alice-in-Wonderland hair, Flo seemed to enjoy the bloody bits of history. 'What have you got for dinner?' Flo's mind was never far off food.

'Cold meat from yesterday. And pickle.'

'Mine's ham, I think. I didn't ask Nell.' Nell was the maid at Flo's house.

Flo hurried off down the stairs as Lizzie hung back for one girl then another to say quiet things to Miss Mitchell – until the last had gone and the mistress turned away to pick up her books.

'Miss Mitchell, excuse me . . .'

'Eliza.'

'Miss Mitchell, I wanted . . . I wondered . . .'

'Yes?' The books were gathered; Miss Mitchell was gathered, her eyes were asking a question.

'Women.' No, the words weren't coming to her by magic; she'd dried up already. 'This isn't about the lesson . . .'

'It sounds not, if it's about women. Parliament's always been about men.' Miss Mitchell made the books comfortable against her bosom, waited.

'Women get treated badly sometimes, don't they? And I thought – what should women do about it? About the way they're badly treated?' Lord, if this had been a composition she'd have been crossing out furiously and starting again.

Miss Mitchell's eyes had opened a little wider, and now she nodded slowly. 'As we find all around us, Eliza, women in society are regarded by men as belonging to a lesser species. The world is run by men for men.' She put her books back on to the desk. 'And that can only be changed *by* women.' She looked hard at Lizzie.

'I agree, ma'am.'

'Is that something that excites you? Your work is good, but you're very quiet in my lessons.' The mistress put her head slightly to one side. 'I'm waiting to find out about the real Eliza Parsons.'

'Some things aren't always what they look like. Or people.' Could she get to her mother's troubles this way?

'I know you as a thoughtful girl, your written work shows clear thinking . . .'

'It's just there are things going on that are downright wrong, and something needs to be done about it.' There! She couldn't have said it more bluntly than that.

Miss Mitchell looked as if she were weighing up some ifs and buts. 'I wonder if you'd like to read a little women's literature that I find helpful? And I don't mean *Jane Eyre*. I mean modern political writing. If that would interest you, I can lend you some.'

'Thank you, Miss Mitchell. It would.' Just to keep the door open.

'Good. That's very good. Then come to the staff common room at the end of school.' The mistress picked up her books again. 'With coal strikes and transport strikes, trade union actions and civil unrest generally, there's been much going on. But it's what women do that will change the country, that's my belief.' She picked up her books. 'Enough! Off you go, Eliza.'

Lizzie – wondering whether she'd just opened a jewellery case or Pandora's box – went to the lockers to get her sandwiches. She avoided Flo by taking them to the loggia instead of the form room, but when she ate them they seemed to have no taste at all and she couldn't tell whether they were beef, ham and pickle, or so much pap. Which was the mixed-up state she was in, without a doubt.

Chapter Four

When Lizzie got home her mother wasn't in – which was very unusual. She banged the knocker and looked through the letter box but the passage was empty and the kitchen door shut. Where could she be? The Mission Hall sometimes had a spring clean or a sale of work, but Lizzie always knew about them and the key was left with next door. She knocked there, and Mrs Farmer was in – with little Annie in her arms.

'It's you, Lizzie. Are you all right?'

'Yes, thank you. But Mum's not answering the door and I wondered if she's given you the key.'

'No, love. You sure she's not in?' She jiggled Annie, who puked.

'I don't think she is.'

'Not out the back?'

'I don't know.'

'Come into the passage.' Mrs Farmer went to check

through her scullery window. 'Can't see her. No sign. Try again, in case she was in the House of Commons when you knocked . . .'

'I'll give it another go. Thanks, Mrs Farmer.'

And this time, Lizzie's door was opened – by her flustered mother, still wearing her hat.

'Sorry, lamb, I cut it fine. I've just this minute got in . . .' She looked fairly normal apart from the fluster, and her smile seemed real enough. 'I was down at the pond – feeding that blessed cake to the ducks. Our birds wouldn't touch it.'

'The same as Dad.' Lizzie hadn't meant to say that but it came out. Even so, her mother smiled.

'Your father's got a taxing job. Those union men in the Arsenal don't make his life easy.'

Lizzie let that talk die; she hung up her things and took out her homework.

'Any more about your poem, Lizzie?'

'No, and there's nothing in here yet –' she tapped her temple – 'never mind on paper.'

'It'll come. Keep thinking about it – what sorts of things inspire you to feel strongly about.' Her mother was taking her writing box down from the alcove. 'You know, we do a lot of writing while we're asleep. I've got a letter for number thirty-eight that's a bit of a fret. If I write it as she wants she'll be badly misunderstood, so I'm leaving it for tomorrow. I'll do something bread-

and-butter meanwhile.' She set out her things. 'We'll share the table when I've made us a cup of tea.'

Lizzie put her homework on her own side, one eye on her mother filling the kettle. She seemed fine today, just like before, although a long way from Christmas at Aunt Elsie's over the water, doing 'The City Waif' with a smudge of soot on her cheeks. Lizzie loved the twinkle in her eyes, which must have been what she was like all the time before she was married.

'What were the respective roles of Thomas Fairfax and Colonel Thomas Pride in the formation of the Rump Parliament?'

Lizzie turned to chapter four in her history book and started making notes, wishing she'd paid more attention in class. But her mind was no more on history tonight than it had been then, and tucked into the back of her book was the folded newspaper Miss Mitchell had given her. Another quick look into the scullery and she slid it out as if it was part of her homework.

The front page of Votes for Women showed a picture of Joan of Arc on a horse, holding her sword aloft. Inside – and Lizzie could take only the quickest of looks – there was a cartoon where three men in togas seemed to be mocking a woman in a Joan of Arc helmet. But on a closer look the woman was a suffragette ready to throw an apple at the three 'Greeks' – clearly politicians – and she was saying, *'Now, let me see, which of these three is my best friend, that I may hurl the apple at him?'* Lizzie didn't understand what it meant, but hadn't someone classical had to choose between three goddesses? So was it all about things turned topsy-turvy?

She hid the newspaper as the hot water went into the teapot and her mother came in with two cups and saucers, ready milked and sweetened, and with not a drip spilt by shaking hands.

'Thanks, Mum.'

'Biscuit, lamb?'

'Please.'

They both set to work; her mother with a letter, Lizzie with the Rump Parliament – but it was hard to stick with it. That Votes for Women newspaper had looked nothing like the papers in the school library. This was like something naughty. She wondered what her mother would think of it. Would it make her sit up? Would anything? She looked so serene and contented, even when she was frowning over this word or that, and the same as before, that calm face made last night's dreads seem impossible. They smiled across at each other, both working away – until the front door slammed and Lizzie heard her dad coming in from work.

Things changed. He always came in like the man in charge, and her mother would cover her papers and look meekly up at him.

'I'll warm up the pot, Jack.'

'You can warm up my supper, too. When a man's done the day's work I've just done he's ready to be fed, *I* can tell you.' He looked over Lizzie's shoulder, patted her on the head. 'Well done, girl.'

And she was grateful that Miss Mitchell's newspaper was well out of sight. Think of the trouble there'd be if he ever set eyes on that. Union men wouldn't come into it . . .

'Did you read the newspaper I gave you?' Miss Mitchell took Lizzie aside in the bustle of the lower corridor. This wasn't a history day and Lizzie hadn't had time to read much of her Votes for Women, but the mistress seemed keen to know.

'It made me feel proud, ma'am, and a bit brave, like Joan of Arc. The Greek cartoon was very good.'

She had said the right thing. Miss Mitchell put a hand on her shoulder, leaned forward and looked intently at her. 'I'm so pleased, Lizzie.' Her voice was almost a whisper. And she'd said *Lizzie,* not *Eliza*. 'We'll talk some more . . .' She went off to her classroom, leaving Lizzie with the nicest feeling in her stomach she'd ever had.

'Are you all right? It's arithmetic, upstairs.' Flo picked up Lizzie's bag from where it had slipped off her shoulder. 'You look hipped.'

But she didn't feel hipped, she felt happy. Things had been quiet last night, no worries. Soon after tea her father had gone out for a 'wet', probably with someone from the Arsenal, come in late, and followed her and her mother up to bed without an atmosphere. But the real situation hadn't changed and Lizzie felt pleased that she'd spoken to Miss Mitchell on Monday. '*We'll talk some more . . .*' A conversation about Votes for Women with Miss Mitchell would be very special – and it might make it easier to talk to her about her mother. And that was the point of it all, wasn't it?

It was the next day after history, although it made for another tricky moment with Flo. As their marked homework was given out Miss Mitchell kept her grip on Lizzie's exercise book, holding her there as she went to take it. 'I'd like to have a word at the end of school.'

'Yes, Miss Mitchell.'

'Come to me here, then, in my room.'

'Yes, Miss Mitchell.'

The book was let go and Lizzie moved on, with Flo close behind.

'What does she want?'

'I don't know.'

'After school?' Flo pulled a sour face, a look Lizzie disliked. Normally Flo was a pretty, round-faced girl with natural curls and big brown eyes, but her sour face turned her into the Duchess in *Alice in Wonderland.* 'Are you in trouble? What did you get for your homework?' Flo was taking the book from Lizzie, and Lizzie had to let her have it. It was all to the good if Flo thought it was about schoolwork.

But it was a humbler all the same – Miss Mitchell had given her only five out of ten for her Rump Parliament homework. '*Not your finest hour, Eliza. Have you been concentrating? Disappointing.*'

Lizzie's insides dived. Miss Mitchell would have changed her mind about what she wanted to say to her. She'd been let down by a distracted and swollen-headed girl who'd been treated a little differently and her trust had been misplaced. A girl who normally got eights and nines for her homework had thrown something on to paper because she thought she was someone special.

'That's why she wants to see you. Five's terrible for you.' Flo didn't look quite so Duchess now.

'What did you get?' Lizzie didn't want to know, but it was called for.

Flo opened her book. It was seven out of ten and, '*A fair grasp of the situation but too many quotes from the textbook. The point is for you to understand.*'

'That's all right, Flo. You didn't disappoint.' Lizzie felt the word stabbing into her. She had disappointed Miss Mitchell.

'Would you like to come home for tea next week?'

Flo was back to her prettiest now. 'Mummy says you may.'

'That'd be nice.' But at the moment there was nothing in the world Lizzie would like less than going to Ashenden House for tea. She wanted to run out of the school and lose herself, get away from everything and everyone. Why couldn't just one part of her life be as laid out on a plate as Flo's? Why had God picked out Lizzie Parsons to be all jumbled-up inside?

She knocked on the history room door, her heart thumping to match her knuckles on the woodwork.

'Come in.'

Miss Mitchell was sitting up at her desk on her high stool eating an apple, sculpting it with a small knife.

Lizzie tried to get this over quickly. 'I'm very sorry, Miss Mitchell.'

'About what?'

'My homework.'

'Oh, that. We all have our off-days.' The mistress put her apple aside. 'So, you appreciated the cartoon of the Greek gods – Grey, Haldane and Lloyd George – being mocked by a militant suffragette . . .?'

Lizzie wanted to sit down. She hadn't betrayed a trust.

'. . . If you had that apple in your hand, to which of the three politicians would you throw it?'

Lizzie knew she mustn't risk disappointing her again. She was being tested, and she'd better get more than five out of ten. The trouble was, one politician was like another to her, the only one she'd heard of was the Prime Minister – Lord Asquith. But she was rescued by a saying of her mother's. '*Tell the truth and shame the devil.*'

'It's not like playing Tinker, Tailor, Soldier, Spy, is it, Miss? I'd have to read about each of them because I don't know enough to pick and choose. I suppose they all have different views about women and the vote . . .?'

Miss Mitchell laughed. 'Not altogether, Lizzie. But you're on the right track. What else took your eye?'

Desperately, Lizzie tried to call up something from those flicked-through pages. She'd had another quick look in her bedroom, her ears pricked for the sound of the stairs, then hidden the paper at the back of her wardrobe and hadn't got back to it.

'It's good that New Zealand women can vote.' She'd seen a headline about that.

'Isn't it? And Australian. Examples that should shame Mr Asquith.' Miss Mitchell had relaxed, head in hand, leaning on an elbow.

'And . . .' Again Lizzie opened her mouth before knowing what she was going to say.

'Yes?'

'Those advertisements.' On some of the pages

there had been women's fashions from the big shops. 'That's by the way, ma'am, but I did like the look of those posh dresses.'

'Well, don't think we can all afford them. Not poor schoolmistresses like us.' She smiled and came away from her desk to give Lizzie a hug around the shoulders. 'We're as poor as church mice.'

Lizzie felt a different person. This wasn't Miss Mitchell the schoolmistress with Eliza Parsons the pupil, this was two people talking about the world.

'And now you must get home – but a question before you go.' Miss Mitchell went to the classroom door and stood with her hand on the handle, keeping the door closed. 'I've been wondering . . .'

'Yes?'

'Are you doing anything special on Saturday afternoon?'

It caught Lizzie's breath. 'I don't know.' What was this about? There were no school events that she knew of. 'I can find out,' she mumbled.

'Yes, please find out and let me know tomorrow. And never mind if you're busy, it's just a thought.'

'No, ma'am.'

'Off you go, then.' Miss Mitchell opened the door a crack, looked along the corridor before widening it. 'And I'd be pleased if this little tête-à-tête were our secret.'

'Of course, ma'am.'

The door was shut quickly and Lizzie went to the top of the stairs – where for a split second she thought she might go head over heels down them. She didn't know who she was any more. She was being treated very specially, and that was tremendously exciting, but was it right for a pupil and a teacher to have a secret between them? And a secret from whom? Yes, from the other girls and the mistresses, but from her mother and father, too? And why did Miss Mitchell need to know about Saturday afternoon?

She walked home in a jumble of school and Miss Mitchell and her mother and father – and as she passed where she'd walked with Joe Gibson last Sunday he came into things as well, a boy who seemed very nice but got a bit hot under the collar. She passed a house with a sleeping baby in a bassinet outside: no cares in the world, nothing in its head – and especially no thoughts about things like politics and men and women and next Saturday.

Oh, Lord, what a state she was in! Why couldn't she be like that baby again?

'Which one is Miss Mitchell? Is she the poem one?'

'No, Dad, that's Miss Abrahams. Miss Mitchell's history.'

Lizzie had left asking her question until teatime

when her father was home – because if she got an answer from her mother which was contradicted by her father there'd be an argument – whereas with the three of them together it would be more like a family discussion.

'What's it all about? Why did she ask?'

Her father had come in from work whistling – something must have pleased him – and then he'd eaten a good tea of fish cakes and mash so the atmosphere was right.

'Is it a school event of some sort, lamb?'

'Give the girl a chance to answer.'

Lizzie didn't know why Miss Mitchell had asked if she was free on Saturday, and she'd been hopelessly trying to think of a reason ever since. Was it something to do with school? Or about the Votes for Women people? Or was it something with Miss Mitchell on their own? But she'd got to give an answer pretty quickly.

'We've been doing the Rump Parliament in history. It could be a public lecture, or something. They take girls to those sometimes, at the Blackheath Halls.'

'Rump! Hah!' Her father was definitely in one of his good moods. 'That's parliament, for you, sums it up – all sitting on their rumps! I could give you a lecture on those fat backsides, madam.'

'Has she asked anyone else you know?' Her mother was keeping to the point.

Lizzie felt herself getting hot. How secret was secret? 'She might have. I'm not sure.'

Her father fished his pipe from his pocket. 'Well.' He opened his tobacco tin. 'It's school. And it's a mistress from Greenfield High School doing the asking.' His voice echoed the pride he'd had in Lizzie getting her scholarship. They waited while he filled his briar, lit it, and after a couple of puffs gave his decision. 'You tell your Miss Malcolm –'

'Miss Mitchell.'

'You tell Miss Mitchell you could be free according to what it's for.' He looked around the table. 'Is that fair, or is it unfair?'

'It's very fair, Jack.'

'Yes, Dad. Thanks.'

'Because I never got asked to do nothing on a Saturday by any of my teachers.'

'Nor me. Not for anything.'

'I had a teacher called Miss Malcolm,' Jack Parsons said to a wreath of smoke. 'You wouldn't want to meet her on a dark night.' He laughed but without humour. 'She could make you jump just with the look in her eyes.' He had an expression on his face that Lizzie had never seen. 'I'd get my own back on her if I ever had the chance.' Her mother gave him a very worried look.

A little embarrassed, Lizzie started clearing the table. Well, he hadn't said a definite 'no', and that was good. Now she just had to wait until tomorrow to know what Saturday afternoon could be all about. So she was helpful, and diligent with her homework, and went up to bed at the first time of asking.

But – Miss Mitchell, her mother and father, Joe Gibson, Miss Mitchell and Miss Mitchell and Miss Mitchell . . . Again that night, sleep was very hard to come by for a girl who was in a bit of a stew.

Chapter Five

Claude Smollett's shop sold groceries and hardware, satisfying most household wants from ham to hammers. Smollett giving 'tick' made it popular, allowing his poorer customers to get food through the week until payday – at a cost. Presiding behind one counter he supervised the grocery side of the shop, while the hardware was overseen by a dry stick of a man called Ernie Smith, with Joe Gibson assisting both.

Smollett was a biggish man, dressed as if for business but without the city jacket. A long apron covered the top button of his waistcoat down to his ankles while black oversleeves protected his white shirt. His streaks of oiled hair were like lines of ink on his head, and his sharp little stones of eyes gave him the look of a man who needed to be treated with respect.

Joe treated both men with politeness and obedience. Respect – as far as giving it to Smollett went – was another matter. He knew too much to have any of that.

That Tuesday afternoon a customer came in wearing a greasy cap and shabby raincoat, and holding a blue mineral-water bottle. Ernie Smith and Joe were both in the storeroom checking a delivery of gas mantles – so Smollett called the man over to the grocery counter.

'Pint of paraffin, please guv'nor.'

Smollett wiped his hands down his apron. 'Give it here.' By law paraffin had to be kept outside the shop so it meant a trip to the yard, but as he went through the bead curtain he beckoned Ernie Smith over. 'Watch him, Ernie – see what his game is.' He went outside while Ernie peered through the beads.

Joe came up behind him. 'What's going on?'

'Ssssh!'

At one end of Smollett's counter a Dundee cake was sitting under domed glass, and at the other there was a stack of open egg boxes, twelve-by-twelves. The man was looking from one end of the counter to the other as if he were weighing something up. He had a thin face with a slit nostril and his hands were twisted with arthritis, but still they managed to do what he wanted. After a quick look around the shop he lifted an egg from the top of the stack and slipped it into the left pocket of his raincoat. Another egg went swiftly into the right pocket. He took a quick look at the curtain, then a second egg went into the left pocket, and a second into the right. Then he dropped his hands and stood waiting like any patient customer.

'What's he up to?' Smollett was behind Ernie Smith.

'Two eggs gone into each pocket.'

'The blighter! I thought I'd had him in before. Well, let's give him a bit more rope to hang himself.' Smollett stayed where he was.

After another keen look at the curtain, the man put another egg into each pocket and stood there humming again. Now Smollett went through with the bottle of paraffin. 'Got the stopper?' In a careful contortion the man fished a stopper from his trouser pocket. Smollett corked the bottle and put it on to the counter, coming around it and facing the man. 'That'll be one-an'-three.'

'*How much*, guv'nor? For a pint of blue paraffin?'

'No, my friend, for a pint of blue paraffin an' six eggs. Three in this pocket' – and Smollett gave a mighty smack of his hand on one pocket – 'an' three in this one,' and he hit the other even harder, knocking the man sideways. Even from where he was, Joe could hear the crunch of eggshell.

The man got his balance back and rushed out of the shop, the yellow of the eggs seeping through his tatty raincoat.

'Ha!' Smollett waggled his fat nose. 'He won't try that trick again.'

Joe came through with a box of gas mantles. 'I think that was a really measly thing to do.' He stood facing Smollett.

'Quite right. Cheap little thief. But I had him! Ha! Worth it for a few eggs. I had a feeling he'd tried a dodge like that before, same slit in the nose.'

Joe's face was reddening. 'No, what was measly was what *you* did.' He ruffled his hair nervously, and his voice came out high. 'I've seen him. He lives rough down near Plumstead Station. He's a real sad item. Half-a-dozen eggs'd get him a night in a dosshouse.'

Shocked, Smollett spread his hands in a 'what-else?' gesture.

'You could've told him to put them back.'

Smollett looked as if he might smack a tray of eggs over Joe's head. 'You soft little mouse! You weasel!' He snorted down his nose. 'If he's down an' out there's the workhouse. Why should I feed the beggar! What the hell's wrong with you?'

The shop bell rang as a customer opened the door but Joe stood his ground – just for a second or so, before plonking the box of mantles on the counter. 'Came in to tell you. This dozen's all smashed,' and he went back outside to check the rest.

At the end of the history lesson Lizzie got up from her desk very slowly. 'I'll catch up with you,' she told Flo.

'I'll wait.'

'No, I'll catch you up.'

Flo pulled a little pussy face and went out of the room.

'Yes, Eliza?' The mistress sounded straighter than yesterday.

'I asked my parents about Saturday, Miss Mitchell . . .'

'And what did they say?'

'I could be free, they said, depending on what it's for.'

Miss Mitchell looked a little surprised. 'Didn't I say?'

'No, ma'am.'

'Well, it's not a mystery.' She started tidying her books on the desk. 'We have a shop in Catford. The Women's Social and Political Union. We sell the *Votes For Women* newspaper and a selection of books from the Women's Press; also scarves and brooches and other paraphernalia.'

Lizzie nodded.

'And it would be good to have a younger person helping with sales and so on. A fresh face amongst the regulars. I've left literature in the common room for the sixth-formers but they're more concerned with their Intermediate examinations – as of course they should be. But this Saturday we're expecting a special visitor and a good turnout. Sylvia Pankhurst, no less.'

'Oh?'

'You know who she is, don't you?'

Lizzie didn't. 'I've certainly heard her name . . .'

'She's the daughter of Emmeline Pankhurst. You've heard about her of course?'

'Of course.'

'She'll attract a fair number. It's been advertised among the local membership, so a quick girl to help with sales will be a boon. Well?' She looked quite business-like at Lizzie.

'What time would you want me, Miss Mitchell?'

'We're shut in the morning preparing, so two until closing time would be useful. Do you think you'll be able to come if you say it's for the WSPU?'

'I'll ask my parents, but I think they'll say yes.' She knew her father wouldn't but she was ready to lie to him. To do something special with Miss Mitchell would be worth a little twist of the truth . . .

'I should appreciate an answer tomorrow.' Which sounded very formal, but Miss Mitchell's eyebrows had arched, as if she was asking a favour.

'Yes, ma'am. I'll bring you one.' Lizzie sounded confident – but she walked clumsily away kicking one foot against the other.

Flo was waiting outside the classroom. 'You're getting on the right side of her, aren't you?'

'How am I?' Had Flo heard everything? Had the door been open?

'That "disappointing" on your homework – you're

trying to show her you're not a dimwit after all.' Flo laughed. 'Which you're not, of course. Come on, Lizpot. It's PT next. You can show Sergeant Feather how high you can jump.'

And arm in arm they went to the gymnasium, Lizzie thinking she was jumping quite high enough already.

'It's a sort of Bring and Buy.'

Her father was late getting in from work, which was happening more and more recently; but he seemed in a good mood – something was going well at the Arsenal.

'A Greenfield school sale?' He always said 'Greenfield' and 'school' as if they were words from the Bible.

'Miss Mitchell's doing the organising.' Which wasn't altogether a lie.

'Do *we* have to bring or buy something?'

Help! 'No, not you. And not me, I'm doing the selling.' She didn't want them thinking of going along. 'It's only for the old girls of the school – and their families.'

'Very clicky.'

'But the funds will help the cause. You know, the old girls' cause.'

'So, where is this, up at the school meadows, I suppose?' Her father hooked his thumbs into the loops of his belt.

'I'm not sure. We're meeting at the school at two

o'clock.' She was making this up but there was no other way.

Her parents looked at one another – Alice non-committal until Jack started nodding his head. 'I don't see why not. So long as you don't mess up the change you give 'em and get cashiered from the regiment. *Cashiered!* Ha!' At which they all laughed until her father began humming a saucy music-hall tune, which had words that were never sung in the house.

Lizzie was in her summer jacket and boater; Miss Mitchell had frowned at the mention of school uniform. She met Lizzie on Woolwich Common and they took two trams to Catford.

'You'll know your own way another time. It's not complicated.'

'Yes, ma'am.' Lizzie was lifted by the thought of a next time – which was suddenly raised aloft by a real surprise.

'Not "ma'am" when we're about like this, Lizzie, and I'd prefer not "Miss Mitchell" either. Outside Greenfield I'm Charlotte.'

'Very well.' Lizzie didn't know how she kept her voice so steady. Miss Mitchell's Christian name wasn't a secret, but to be told to use it stopped her breath. She could just see Flo doing her Duchess face if she ever let on.

Miss Mitchell – Charlotte – paid the fares and got them off the second tram at Rushey Green, walking them up a side road to a shop in the middle of a small terrace. It was hung outside like a fairground booth with swathes of purple, white and green curtaining in loops beneath the upstairs windowsills. The shop wasn't big – single-fronted with 'VOTES FOR WOMEN' whitewashed on the window – but on the wide pavement in front of it there were trestle tables with clusters of people looking at all manner of books and pamphlets. A couple of women had small medals pinned to their coats but Lizzie was too polite to look down at their inscriptions. From what Lizzie had seen of suffragettes in the school library newspapers she'd expected everyone to be dressed in hats and coats from top London shops, and some were, but there were poorer people here too – and they weren't all women. A few men were browsing, and across the road, Lizzie could see a group of youths jostling among themselves behind a coal man's horse and cart. Were they plucking up the courage to come over and take a closer look?

Inside, the shop was long and narrow. At the far end was a platform done up like a concert-party stage with a backdrop of Joan of Arc riding her horse in front of the Houses of Parliament, just like the front of the *Votes for Women* newspaper. A polished counter ran down one side of the shop, and trestle tables were on the other, with expensive items on both – Bibles and other better-bound books, brooches, necklaces and bracelets. On display rails hung coats in purple embellished with green, and coats in green embellished with purple, together with all manner of flags, draperies, cushions, embroideries and handkerchiefs, most of them embroidered with 'WSPU' in one or other of the colours.

'Purple for dignity, white for purity and green for hope.' Miss Mitchell was always the teacher. A cluster of brooches took Lizzie's eye, one in particular like her mother's amber pendant – a glass oval with three words embedded: *Res Non Verba*. 'Deeds not words! The motto of our cause.' She led Lizzie through the shop-full of people, which was bustling and yet calm. There were calls and laughs, a gentle tone and a civilised jostling in which Lizzie wouldn't have been surprised to see her headmistress, Miss Tudor Hart – and her own polite and pleasant mother wouldn't have been so very out of place. But where were they going, and what was she supposed to do? The counter and the tables had women serving behind them already.

'Come on, Lizzie.' Miss Mitchell took her hand and steered her to the far end of the shop: Lizzie Parsons holding hands with a schoolmistress! On the way through she was introduced as 'Lizzie Parsons, one of my girls.' 'Lizzie Parsons – she's here to help.' 'Meet Lizzie Parsons, keen for the cause.' There were smiles, 'jolly goods', a thumbs-up and a clenched fist.

'I've set us up here.' They were in front of the platform where a half-yard width of black cloth ran across the boards from one side to the other. Miss Mitchell lifted it off and now Lizzie could see what she would be selling: gloves, forty or fifty pairs of cotton and silk and leather gloves, some green and purple but mostly white and black. Miss Mitchell tied a money bag around her own waist. 'We'll both use mine. And it's one-and-sixpence for the cotton, three-and-nine-pence for the leather, and five shillings for the silk. I'm sure you can tell between cotton and silk, Lizzie?'

It took a couple of seconds for Lizzie to decide how to answer. 'Yes, Charlotte,' she said with a very straight face.

'Bravo! So let's –' But Charlotte Mitchell didn't need to declare her glove counter open, it was thronged already.

'Wendy! Gloves! And in the colours, too.'

Lizzie was engulfed, twisting this way and that as women chose gloves, discarded them, went for others, and asked the prices. In no time she was showing and selling like a true glover, darting to Charlotte Mitchell with the money, back with the change, the two of them checking each other's transactions now and then like friends at a church fête; and in quick exchanges in between, Charlotte told her about who was who and what was what.

The stock sold well, and two hours went by very

quickly; until a quiet word came for them to pack up; and when Lizzie had helped to wrap the unsold gloves in tissue paper and put them into a small suitcase, Charlotte Mitchell shook her hand, and held on to it. 'Well done, Lizzie, you were a huge help – and wonderful to work with. You're going to be a truly welcome addition to our ranks.'

'Thank you, I enjoyed it,' but Lizzie's hand wasn't dropped until she'd got out another 'Charlotte'.

'Votes for Women!'

Lizzie turned to look up as a tall woman in a beribboned hat came on to the platform with a concertina slung around her neck. So this was why they'd had to clear the platform. She placed her feet in a performing stance and without any introduction she played a long chord and the shop went quiet.

'That's Vera Lytton the actress,' Charlotte whispered.

The actress played the first bars of 'The Vicar of Bray' on her concertina and then to the familiar tune she started to sing in a strong melodious voice.

'*When Good Queen Bess was on the Throne*
Three hundred years ago, Sir
For forty years she reigned alone
As everyone must know, Sir
She laboured for her country's sake
And no one questioned then, Sir

The right of England's Queen to make

The laws of England's men, Sir.'

From the audience came murmurs of quiet agreement with the words.

'But this is true, they will maintain

As true as holy writ, Sir

That whatsoever woman may do

To vote she is not fit, Sir.'

Everyone in the shop knew the chorus – except Lizzie – who hummed it instead. Holding the audience with her eyes Vera Lytton marched stage left and turned sharply, coming back to the centre:

'But still today the tale goes on

Just as in days gone by, Sir

Although three hundred years are gone

You still may hear the cry, Sir

That though to work in every –'

But suddenly the cry to be heard came from the street – loud shouts by male voices:

'Get back to your kitchens!'

'Keep out of men's affairs!'

'No brains *in* women – no votes *for* women!'

Then all together in a chorus: 'Take some of your own medicine!' – and lumps of coal came smashing through the shop window, splintering glass all over the shop, with one great sheet crashing to the floor. There were screams and shouts and people rushing for the door to get at the youths. There were cuts and blood and tears as the attackers, a group of youths, ran off shouting insults over their shoulders.

'Stupid women!'

'Keep your place!'

'Fit for three things! Blacking, baking and bedding!'

An elderly man who had chased them and run out of breath came back into the shop. 'They're . . . well on their way . . . but I know . . . who they are.'

'Catford toerags!'

'No . . . I recognised two of them . . . Students from Guy's Hospital.'

'Disgusting!'

'They're not allowed to vote themselves!'

The mood in the shop had changed – but the place was defiant in the clearing-up. The broken window was covered with a nailed tarpaulin; two nurse suffragettes tended to the cut faces and arms; and Charlotte Mitchell gave Lizzie a pair of unsold leather gloves to wear for putting broken glass into a bucket. And only now, it seemed, did anyone remember the guest of honour.

'It's fortunate that Miss Pankhurst wasn't here.'

'Sylvia was in Bethnal Green and Poplar before coming to us. She'll be here later.'

'She can tell her mother what window-breaking does for the cause!' – a comment which started a fierce argument.

'It's divisive,' Charlotte Mitchell said. 'Militancy. Breaking windows. Some want to pursue one course, others another – but we're united as a sex.'

Lizzie was helping to carry the heavy bucket out to the backyard.

'Absolutely.' But she wanted to say some more, something more personal. She wanted to tell Charlotte she'd never spent such an important few hours in her life: the strong feeling here of togetherness, of a common cause. Or rather, *causes,* because there'd been such a strong sense in the shop of them being women as well as suffragettes this afternoon, people determined not to depend on men, whether they got the vote or not.

'I think you should go home now, Lizzie. You've seen the sort of thing that can happen; Votes for Women is no bed of roses, but if today gives you resolve you're going to be a great asset to the cause.'

'You can count upon me, you certainly can.'

'Yes, I think so.' Charlotte gave Lizzie her tram fares home. 'Get your jacket, Lizzie, and I'll see you on Monday.'

Monday, and school. It seemed a different world. She looked Charlotte in the eyes before turning for the door. 'Yes, Miss Mitchell,' she said.

And she was slightly disappointed that Miss Mitchell didn't correct her.

Chapter Six

Joe Gibson stood looking along the High Street, a few yards short of the Plumstead Hall. He had been there for twenty minutes, his head gradually drooping like a tulip without water. Groups of lads and girls passed by him: 'Waiting for Christmas, Joe?' 'Put your cap on the pavement an' give us a song.' 'She'll never come, mate.' He didn't rise to any of them but kept his eyes on the corner she'd come round. The audience going in for *Nero* on the cinematograph dwindled, and finally Joe went towards the closing doors. He took one last look back – and there was a girl coming towards him, walking sedately, looking as if she had all the time in the world. And she had, as far *Nero* was concerned. She went on past the hall and up a side street. He pushed his cap to the back of his head and started walking home – without the spit for a whistle.

* * *

Lizzie's father got into the house at around ten o'clock that night. Lizzie had already told her lies to her mother so they were firm in her head, but she wouldn't need to repeat them. Her father was in a good mood. 'Decent bloke to have a pint with, old Wally Waters.' He went to the scullery to give his hands a good wash.

'Lizzie did well today,' Alice told him. 'She sold a lot of gloves at the school sale.'

'More than a handful? Gloves. Ha!'

'Some were silk, weren't they, Lizzie?'

'White silk, black silk . . .'

'None red, I hope. No scarlet ladies among the old girls?'

'Jack!'

He laughed and gave the roller towel a good pull. 'Anyhow, it's time you got to bed, madam.'

Alice took a pork pie from the larder. 'Would you like this, Jack, with a cup of tea?'

'I would, thank you. But not cold. They was cold in the Old – in the old Woodman. Warm it through, will you?'

Alice found a skillet and put it on the stove; while Lizzie said her goodnights and went upstairs to bed. Not to sleep, though; her head was filled with a jumble of memories that shot from one thing to another like a frantic slide show: sitting on the tram next to Miss Mitchell; being in the suffragette shop with all those sure and certain women; seeing those gloves being tried on all those different hands, rough and smooth, old and young, ringed and bare; her and Miss Mitchell each delving into the money pouch, laughing when one of them got the change wrong, shimmying round each other to serve. But apart from the terrible scare of the window caving in, the most vivid memory of all was the thrill she'd had when Miss Mitchell asked to be called Charlotte – the surprise of her life, like suddenly growing up on that tram ride. But everything clouded when she thought about the end of the afternoon. When it was time to go home Charlotte seemed to be quite content to be Miss Mitchell, which could have waited until Monday. So all in all Lizzie didn't know whether she was up or down or both, neither like this nor like that – a feeling of deep uncertainty that was like an aching snake in her stomach. Which told her that nothing had really changed, didn't it?

She turned over in bed and tried thinking of something else altogether – something not to do with Miss Mitchell. And out of nowhere came Joe Gibson. In the excitement of the day he'd been pushed from her mind, and this evening she'd been too focused on keeping her lies in line to think of anyone but herself. So, had Joe waited for her down at the Plumstead Hall? Had he given it until half-past six and then gone in – with the Ascension lads, or one of the pretty girls? She turned over again. Yes, he would have gone in, because he hadn't expected her to go, not by the way he'd walked away from the pond. He'd tried to be bright before they parted, but his head had gone down after his rant about Smollett – he was upset with himself.

And what if he'd turned around and seen her throw his flowers into the pond? How would that have made him feel?

Another twist of her sheets, another pummel of her pillow, but Joe stayed in her head as she remembered his angry face as he went on about the putty under Smollett's scales, and that old woman being bullied over her tick. And to her surprise she suddenly found herself sitting up against the headboard with her arms folded tight. *Because Joe Gibson was different, wasn't he?* He was a miles better boy than those medical students who'd shouted their filth about women. The way he felt about Smollett cheating a widow was just the way those women in the Catford shop would feel. So was he at fault for getting angry? No – just the opposite. He was entitled. What Miss Mitchell and those women were doing was very important – women had rights to equality in everything – and Joe Gibson's feelings about life were the same as theirs. So he had to feel good about showing them, not bad.

It was late, and her room was getting chilly. She lay down again, pulled up the coverlet and stared at the ceiling, her eyes wide open. She turned to one side, turned to the other, and turned on to her back again. Well, she decided, she was going to find Joe Gibson as soon as she could and offer to meet him soon. She owed him that – didn't she?

And besides, he was someone of her own age whose name didn't change according to where he was, or where they went together.

Her world wasn't up to much on Monday, as she'd expected. It started with history, and when she walked into the classroom there was not the slightest sign from Miss Mitchell that Saturday had happened. Of course she hadn't expected one, but she was still disappointed when there wasn't even a glance in her direction.

Flo loved every second of the forty minutes – at last they'd got through the Long and the Short Parliaments and the trial of Charles the First. Now came his execution, and Miss Mitchell did dramatic justice to it.

'However history has judged Charles the First, he was certainly a very brave man,' she told them. 'He asked for two shirts to wear beneath his doublet and cloak so that he shouldn't shiver in the cold of January – else the crowd might think him afraid. And he helped the executioner to strike an accurate blow on his neck by tucking his long hair under his cap.'

Flo growled in her throat as she scribbled a note.

'And it was a clean cut – by a skilled executioner wearing a mask in case the people turned against him afterwards. Charles's lead-lined coffin in Windsor Castle was opened a hundred years ago and the skill of the cut was verified . . .'

Every face in the room had the same look upon it, how gruesome to open the king's coffin – except Flo's who was nodding and wanting more.

Miss Mitchell dropped her voice. 'And what was revealed that day was that after the execution – after his severed head had been held up for the crowd to see – it was put back in place and sewn on to his neck again . . .'

Flo's pencil snapped – not just the lead, the whole pencil.

Lizzie's heart had quickened, too. Death. Its chill wasn't new to her. Little Freddie had looked as if he was asleep in his coffin, but when she kissed his forehead it had a coldness she'd never forget.

'So,' Miss Mitchell went on in a drier voice, 'we come to the abolition of the monarchy – passed by the Rump on 17th March 1649 – and the establishment of the Commonwealth of England, which is a most fascinating period in constitutional terms . . .'

But Flo had abandoned the stub of her pencil as history marched on; and although Lizzie dallied slightly at the end of the lesson, Miss Mitchell was occupied with questions as she gathered up her books.

And things didn't get any better. Miss Abrahams said she wanted a word with Eliza after school and Lizzie knew what that would be about: the League of British Girls' Schools' poem, which hadn't come to life yet. Yes, she'd thought about it, but she'd had no ideas, seemed unable to get inspiration anywhere.

'I'm wondering how the poem is coming along, Eliza.' Miss Abrahams was crisp and businesslike.

'The poem? It's all right, ma'am. But it's still more here –' Lizzie tapped her temple – 'than here.' She scribbled in the air.

Miss Abrahams nodded, once – she never nodded twice – and Lizzie's answer seemed to be acceptable. 'Well, *tempus fugit,* and come for a word if it helps. One or two of the others are well on their ways.'

'Yes, Miss Abrahams.'

'And speaking of words, I've found one of these a help when I'm writing school reports.' She took a book from her desk. 'Roget's Thesaurus: it's given me many a variation on "disappointing".' She handed it over. 'Off you go, then. I'll have that back when you're finished with it.' She waved a snappy hand of dismissal.

'Thank you, ma'am.'

Lizzie headed off towards the school exit, but Flo had waited for her. 'I meant to say before – Mama says you should come to afternoon tea one day soon. But not on a Wednesday, that's lacrosse when I'm in the team.'

'And we have Club at the Mission.'

'Mama says strawberry muffins!' Flo ran her tongue around her lips.

'Lovely. I'll ask my dad.'

'And ginger beer.'

'Oooh.' But Lizzie wanted to get away. 'Got to go. Monday!' As if that meant anything.

'See you tomorrow.'

They walked to the end of Greenfield's private road and on to Shooters Hill. Flo went off towards Blackheath while Lizzie went her own way. But not to go home, because when she'd woken that morning she'd known where she was going after school, and she'd have time to do it if she didn't dawdle.

Smollett's Household Provisions was on the tram route and facing Woolwich Common. It had 'High Class Purveyor to the Gentry' painted in gold across its window – and peering through it that afternoon Lizzie could see Joe Gibson up a ladder, wearing such a long apron that he looked ten feet tall. She went into the shop getting a louder jangle from the bell than she wanted. Joe was dusting a top shelf of shopping baskets and tin kettles. She watched him flicking with his feather duster but she was keeping an eye on Smollett, too, who was smiling and bowing to a woman she took to be the gentry mentioned on the window.

'Thank you, madam, greatly obliged.' Smollett had come from behind the counter. 'I shall send them around in the morning.' He showed the gentry out through the door – almost knocking Lizzie aside with his rump.

And Joe was down that ladder like a circus turn. 'Yes, miss? Can I help you?'

'Do you sell toffee?' Lizzie looked around her. Smollett was at the door stroking his fat cheeks.

'You want the confectioner's around the corner, miss. We have to keep to our different trades. Shall I show you the way to Figgs's Sweet Shop?' Joe gave Lizzie a wink and walked her to the door. 'Young lady wants Figgs's,' he told his guv'nor.

'Two minutes, boy. Nell Figgs wouldn't walk someone round to me.'

Joe and Lizzie kept their strangers' faces on until the corner was turned.

'I don't really want toffee. It's too hard to break.'

'No?' He stopped. 'Well, you've broken something, Lizzie Parsons.'

Her head was up in a shot. 'I didn't break a promise. I never said I'd –'

'You broke my dream. Coming in the shop just now. I nearly fell off my ladder.'

'Sorry.'

'Last night, I've just gone off to sleep, Land of Nod, and you come walking in through Smollett's shop door as large as life and pretty as a picture . . .'

'Stop that. What did I buy?'

'I didn't get that far. Smollett said something nasty so I kicked him up the bum and woke myself up.'

Lizzie laughed, shook her head. She couldn't tell with this boy – was he having her on? 'I don't know where you live, so it's the real me who's come here to say sorry for not turning up on Saturday.'

Joe smoothed his apron down but it ruffled up again. 'I can't remember if I went myself. Let me see, Saturday . . .' He mused, then laughed. 'I did go, but I didn't see old *Nero* – I waited outside for a bit, then I went home and beat Gran at cards.'

'I had to go out Saturday afternoon and I got back late.'

'But would you have come if you could?'

Well, there was nothing like being direct. 'Yes. I would, if they'd let me.'

Joe's hair seemed to spike up, all by itself. 'Listen, Smollett's has a half-day on Thursdays . . .'

'Does it? Miss Tudor Hart doesn't give one to me.'

'I could meet you outside the school and walk you home . . .'

'No, I don't think so.' Flo's head would come off as she walked away pretending not to look.

'Tell you what, then, we'll get ourselves a drop of sea air, brace ourselves with a whiff of the briny . . .'

'What?'

'Go across the ferry and back, time for a little talk, and then have a proper walk one Sunday.'

That sounded good to Lizzie. The Free Ferry across to North Woolwich was always a treat whether it was with her friends or with her mother.

'I'll let you know. Where do you live?'

'Garland Road. Number two Rose Cottages.'

'I'll put a note through your letter box.'

Joe shook his head. 'No, not through the door. I love old Gran but she's got a nose long enough for going cockling . . .'

Lizzie laughed. Joe was a sea breeze himself.

'. . . There's a flowerpot by the gate. Put it under there.'

'All right. But you'd better get back to Smollett or you won't just have a half-day off – you'll have all day every day.'

He gave her a serious look. 'And I do come pretty close to that sometimes.'

'Well, try to keep your tin lid on. Now off you go –' she gave him a little push. 'And be good.'

'Good as I can. Cheerio.' With a nod he went his way, kicking his legs against his long apron; and Lizzie went hers, walking fast to get to Sutcliffe Road at a reasonable time. The more normal things were at home, the better – because these days everything else was getting in a proper state.

* * *

She had a small triumph when her father came in from work, later again but in a cheerful mood. She asked if she could go to tea at Flo's one afternoon and he said yes, seeming pleased that a Sutcliffe Road girl should be invited to a high-class house in Blackheath. On the back of that success Lizzie tried to sort one of her problems. The poem. The Poem! It ran in her head like a headline of doom and disaster. The pride of being picked to write something had long gone, and she wished she'd said nothing to her parents about it – because she would have asked Miss Abrahams to be excused. Whenever she sat down to her homework her father would say 'Poetry?' and sometimes she'd nod with a little smile and at others say, 'Not tonight.' But the need to do it was there all the time, like a summer cold that wouldn't go away.

She enjoyed writing. Her essays usually earned good marks, and her poems – where the exercises were to write something in the style of one of the greats – were often read to the class as the way to do them. But the problem she had now was not being able to write in the style of Lizzie Parsons. She could sound like Keats or Wordsworth but she couldn't sound like herself, and for this she had to *be* herself. But what self? She seemed to be a different person every day of the week. If she could just get a line down she'd have a clue and feel better, which might lead somewhere. So that was tonight's aim: to at least sketch out a first line, and maybe two. She sharpened her pencil into the kitchen sink and opened her English exercise book, upside down from the back. And then stared at it, because a blank page is a blank page at either end of a book. Nothing came into her head – although should she be surprised at that? Poetry had been crowded out of it for some time.

She flattened her book again, and just to look busy she wrote any old words on the paper; random thoughts that seemed slightly poetic. '*Summer – flowers in. Trees – life of an oak leaf. Bees – quarrels in the hive. Our street – arguments over children. Watson the rent man – nice to Mum, nasty to next door.*' And from Watson she went to Smollett – '*Bullies. Power. Fairness. Rights. Equality.*' She looked them up in Miss Abrahams's Thesaurus but alternatives weren't much good if they led nowhere as well.

'The poem?' Her mother had sat opposite her at the table.

'How did you know?'

'You're looking as much at the ceiling as the page. But what I used to find was a help . . .'

'There was a young fellow from France –' Her father knocked out his pipe.

'. . .What I found was a help,' her mother repeated, 'was not starting with a rhythm and going down through verse after verse trying to make it fit but jotting down all sorts of words, some linked, some opposites, buzz around an idea – like something you know about, people, things – and let the poem's pattern come later. Go here, go there, go on, go back. Put in. Take away. Dodge about . . .'

'I've started doing a bit of that . . .'

'Well I'm going to dodge about.' Lizzie's father stirred. 'I might go for a stroll and look in at the Woodman for Wally Waters.'

When he'd gone Lizzie became busier. Thinking about Joe and his Mr Smollett, she looked up 'fairness' and found 'social justice', 'equity' and 'fair play' – all possibilities that could lead to other places. She made notes about them all: at school, at home, in factories and shops and on the playing field. She covered a couple of pages, and eventually, blowing out her cheeks, she put away her things and said a big thank you to her mother. She still hadn't got very far with the poem as a poem but she was content to have made something of a start, and being grateful for the peaceful house she went up to bed thinking she'd probably get off to sleep quite quickly tonight.

Unless Joe Gibson kept her awake, of course.

Chapter Seven

The first thing Lizzie did getting to school next day was to find Flo and say she'd like very much to go to tea with her one afternoon. 'A Thursday for preference, if it's convenient for your mother.'

'Any day. Mama says any day except Friday; it's Blackheath Circle on Fridays.'

'Even Thursday of this week?'

'*Parfait*. And Mama says no gifts. You're not to bring flowers or anything.'

'All right.' Lizzie hadn't thought about that, but then Ashenden Park at Blackheath wasn't her world. Joe's cottage would be more like it, though, and already she was composing a note to put under his flowerpot. She and Flo weren't in the same set for French, which gave her a chance next lesson to tug a page from the centre of her exercise book without being quizzed.

Dear Joe,

I can meet you this Thursday at the ferry. I'll be there sometime before six, but wait for me if I'm a bit late. If you aren't there I'll know you couldn't come.

That was the easy bit – but how to sign it at the bottom? 'Yours faithfully'? 'Yours truly'? Definitely not 'Love'. But before the lesson was over she'd finished and folded it: '*In haste – L*'. No kisses, of course. And when it was safe in her pocket she set her face for physics.

Rose Cottages were in a line of four at the top end of Garland Road. Joe didn't live far from her at all; it was just a wonder she'd never bumped into him. But today she didn't want to bump into anyone, especially not his gran, so she walked on the other side of the road to give Joe's cottage a good once-over. Number two was the same as its neighbour, a low building with a window in the roof, like in the country. She listened for the sound of talking or singing, but all she could hear were the cows from the field behind it. Now she walked past on the cottages' side – and there inside the gate of Number two was a flowerpot of freesias. She took a quick look at the parlour curtains, but nothing twitched – so in a sudden stoop she opened the gate, put her note beneath the flowerpot and walked off down the road. And when she was twenty yards away she stopped, turned, and blew a kiss back at the cottage.

So how silly was that?

Flo and Lizzie stood on the bottom bar of the gate to Ashenden House. It seemed a silly thing for girls their age to do but it was fun.

'Ready?'

'Ready.'

Flo let go the latch and the gate swung in a wide arc into a clump of laurels.

'Wooooh!'

'Weeeee!'

The front garden dipped towards the large porch. They smoothed their uniforms and Flo pulled on the bell, which the housemaid quickly answered.

''Lo, miss.'

'Hello, Nell. You remember my friend Eliza?' Nell bobbed. She was a short girl about their age dressed in cap and apron. 'Mama! Lizzie's here.'

The hallway of Ashenden House was dominated by a tall grandfather clock, which Lizzie knew would be important that afternoon.

'How lovely to see you, Eliza.' Mrs Lewis came from the drawing room. No kiss, but a handshake. 'Now, you'll want to wash off the ink of the day, I'm sure.' She waved her hand towards the small cloakroom, which was along a side corridor. Lizzie knew the way. 'Florence, you can use the bathroom.' Mrs Lewis looked like royalty – square face, shoulders, and stance – wearing a silk dress that looked as if it had come from China.

The grandfather clock in the hallway chimed the half hour: half past four. Lizzie went to the cloakroom. Her hair never needed too much attention so all she had to do was splash her face, but she stayed in there awhile. She hadn't been alone all day and she wanted to think. She looked into the mirror – and suddenly pulled a face at herself. What *was* she doing these days? Was she still Lizzy Parsons or was she turning into someone else? She was lying to people left, right and centre; she'd deliberately misled her parents – they knew she was coming here but nothing about afterwards – and when the clock chimed half past five she was going to lie to Mrs Lewis and get away. Where would it all end? Well, not here in the cloakroom. She checked her teeth, straightened her dress and unlocked the door. She had planned this, now she had to see it through.

Flo came down the stairs in a pretty frock.

'That's nice.' But Lizzie was envious. She was going to meet Joe in her school uniform.

'Well, now, I think it's warm enough to take refreshments on the balcony. I hope that suits you, Eliza?'

'That would be very nice, Mrs Lewis, thank you.'

'Then lead on, Florence.'

Flo led the three of them to the back of the house, through the sitting room and on to a balcony, which overlooked Blackheath. The table was laid for afternoon tea with Nell unveiling the cake-stand: two layers of strawberry muffins just as Flo had promised.

'Mmmm!'

'They look delicious. Strawberry jam's my favourite.'

'Then we shall see if it's a good year.' Mrs Lewis waved a hand for Nell to serve them.

Lizzie wasn't worried by the formalities of afternoon tea. Her mother had taught her how to handle cutlery, while Greenfield High taught etiquette. But this jam would have challenged Queen Mary herself. It spread and it ran, and there was an awkward moment when Nell told Mrs Lewis she'd got jam on the end of her nose. 'Thought I'd better say, ma'am.'

'Oh, dear. I must look fit for a circus.'

More jam muffins were offered, while in between mouthfuls Mrs Lewis asked questions about school and Lizzie's family, showing an especial interest in Mr Parsons's work in the Royal Arsenal. 'A hero, I understand from Florence. The Edward Medal, no less.'

'He doesn't say much about it, Mrs Lewis.'

'Heroes don't as a rule.'

The talk went on – this and that, with questions about the mistresses, and Lizzie hoping she wasn't blushing at the mention of Miss Mitchell. And suddenly the grandfather clock was chiming – five o'clock! Was it wrong or had she missed the quarter to? She'd better listen hard for the quarter and the half past. But at least the afternoon tea was moving through and there'd be an end to it; then she could make her excuses for going: her poor mother's nausea and having to help with her father's supper. She accepted another muffin – they needed to be eaten – and took another sip of her ginger beer, the jug going down nicely, too. Which was when Commander Lewis walked on to the balcony, home from the Admiralty. He was a shortish man with a small head and a bristly moustache.

'A chair for me if you please, Nell, and three fingers of best malt – I need a stiffener.'

Lizzie knew something about him from Flo. He was a naval commander who worked near Trafalgar Square and wore a suit instead of a uniform. He was under the First Lord whom the commander didn't like – but that wasn't the cause of his bad mood today.

'Grown women in the Strand, chalking on the pavements like schoolchildren! Giving out their pathetic literature and shouting insults at any passing man!' He held his out hand for his whisky. 'Is that last muffin spoken for, Flossie?'

'No, Daddy, you have it.'

'Bally suffragettes. If they're not smashing windows they're making damned nuisances of themselves in other ways.' He took a gulp of his Scotch.

'This is Eliza, George. Florence's friend from the school.'

'How d'you do, Eliza?' He gave the jam no chance of spreading by opening his mouth wide and sending the muffin in whole. 'Keeping old Flossie in order at the learning shop?'

'It's more the other way around . . .'

'What do they want?' The commander spoke through the muffin. 'The world's gone mad. The PM's got a long and poisonous menu on his agenda – the coal strike, the cotton weavers, the dockers, the Irish problem – in the midst of which, these stupid women want to take up parliamentary time with calls for the right to vote.' He chased the muffin down with his Scotch and held out his glass to Nell. 'How can votes for women be a priority on the PM's plate? You should hear the First Lord on the subject . . .'

'He's not sympathetic to the cause?' Mrs Lewis waved Nell and the whisky decanter away.

'To women? Winston? Certainly not where votes for women is concerned, and I'm with him on that.'

Lizzie was listening hard to this, thinking of Miss Mitchell and the women in the Catford shop. 'What were they chalking, sir?'

'Not hopscotch squares, Eliza. Latin. Bally Latin. "Res Non Verba" – Deeds Not Words – some sort of a motto. And what deeds . . .' He looked round for Nell and the decanter but they had gone. 'Smashing windows, stoning buildings, setting fire to a pillar box, carrying handbags filled with pebbles to throw under police horses' hooves . . .'

'Have some tea.' Mrs Lewis poured him a cup. 'You're getting loud, dear.'

But not so loud to drown the sound of the grandfather clock. The half hour. Half past five. Lizzie had missed the quarter. 'Oh lor', I'm forgetting!' She folded her napkin and stood up, trying to take it slowly. 'Oh, stupid me!'

'What is it, dear?'

'My mother. She was nauseous this morning and there's father's meal to be cooked. I've had such a lovely time I've forgotten all about it, and I think that was half past five. What sort of daughter am I?' It sounded rather sudden and strong, too theatrical, even to herself.

'Then you should go, Eliza. Parlour games can wait for another time.'

Flo became the Duchess as she waited for Lizzie to say her goodbyes, then led her through the house to the hall – with Commander Lewis behind them.

'Nell? Nell? Where are you?' He waved goodbye to Lizzie and found the maid – and the decanter – in the kitchen.

Flo opened the front door. 'Anyway, I hope your ma feels better soon.' She said it with some grace. 'I'm sorry your visit ended up with talk of violent women. They do need putting in their place, don't you think?'

Lizzie managed to be in too much of a hurry to reply. 'Bye, Flo! Thanks ever so much.' She ran through the gateway and crossed the road on to Blackheath, taking a diagonal towards the bus stop for Woolwich. And now she could think of what lay ahead. So was Joe on his early closing, or was Smollett stocktaking or something? Would he be there or wouldn't he? She went fluttery inside at the thought of seeing him again. Or were those butterflies something else – to do with the dishonest way she was behaving these days?

Joe was there, watching the horses and carts coming off the ferry. Tall, with a collarless Russian-style shirt and bare head, he looked like a storybook hero. He waved, and Lizzie ran to him across the ferry approach – so as not to miss the boat, of course.

'Where's your cap?' Joe's hair was dancing in the breeze.

'Lost one in the froth once, not losing another. You'll have to hang on to yours.'

Lizzie's hat was a Greenfield beret, which she crammed into her bag. 'Have you been waiting long?'

'No, got here as this chap docked. Come on.' He

led her on to the pier and along to the boat, which was loading with horses and carts. 'Down we go.' They headed for the promenade deck and a place on the rail just astern of the paddle wheels – no discussion: everyone in search of a thrill on the ferry knew exactly where to stand. Lizzie looked across to the other side of the river, the foreign land that was North Woolwich.

'Shall we go for a quick stroll over there?' Joe's hair was like wheat in the wind as he faced into the water's blow.

Lizzie hung back a little. 'No, straight back on this one. If the other boat's held up I'll get home too late.' The two boats never ran like clockwork, a broken cart axle on one could leave the other boat in midstream, waiting to get in. 'This is only a quick hello.'

'Hello.'

'Hello.'

They both laughed, but Joe suddenly went serious. 'Do you think you're taking a chance on me, Lizzie Parsons? Is this only a quick hello to make sure you like me?'

'That's a funny thing to say.' But there was truth in it – she'd had serious second thoughts about his rant over Smollett, throwing him into her favour; but had she been wrong? Was that partly why she was here, to make sure? 'What sort of a chance would I be taking? Chance means gambling and we don't gamble.'

'I gamble – but not with money.'

'Oh?'

'I'm always gambling with my job.'

'Like spilling paraffin?'

'No, the way Smollett carries on – if I said the stuff he needs saying to him he'd kick me out, straight off. Right's right, I reckon, and wrong's wrong the world over, but I'll make it for something really worth risking.'

Oh, yes. She liked him. There weren't a lot of boys she knew who were like that. 'Don't cut off your nose to spite your face, Joe. Keep your mouth shut until you've got something else lined up – or you'll get your ticket shoved in it!'

He laughed at that and rubbed his chin, seemed about to say more but she didn't let him. 'I could meet you on Sunday if you like,' she said. That should put paid to talk of her taking a chance.

'About the same time as before?'

'Around four o'clock suits me.'

He smiled, taking the reprimand.

That was settled, then. The hooter sounded. The stacks coughed black smoke, the deck shuddered and as the paddle wheels turned, the *Gordon* started moving away from the pier. And the water on their side didn't disappoint. As the boat picked up speed, the wheel turned faster and faster, gathering pace and force to lather the brown water of the Thames into a scary frothing white torrent. Lizzie stared at it, hypnotised like always, her heart racing and her stomach rolling and the thought of falling into it making her dizzy. Sometimes on the way over to Aunt Elsie's she and her mother would stand here clutching each other, with the story told every time of the woman who threw herself into the churning river wearing a thick fur coat on a summer's day. 'To make sure she sank, Lizzie, to make sure the poor soul sank.'

Joe's eyes were boggling. 'Imagine falling into that, Lizzie – doesn't bear thinking about!'

'Or what about being pushed in?' Into her head came one of her mother's recitations from Dickens. She did it for Joe.

'*No eye beheld when William plunged*
Young Edmund in the stream;
No human ear but William's heard
Young Edmund's drowning scream.
But never could Lord William dare
To gaze on Severn's stream;
In every wind that swept its waves
He heard young Edmund's scream . . .'

She made the sound of a troll and pulled the melodramatic face her mother did.

'Stop! You're scaring me.' But Joe was laughing.

With the boat vibrating from bow to stern Joe pulled Lizzie away, down to the lower deck where they could go inside and stare at the starboard engine. Only a thin rail separated them from those great rotating pistons – monstrous things with a life of their own, and very frightening. Again Lizzie's heart thumped her breast. But Joe's arm was around her waist, so she put her arm around his, and they stood there like that all the way to North Woolwich as if they were saving each other from grisly deaths.

The pistons slowed, the boat bumped alongside the pier, they went up on deck and walked off up the ramp to come straight back down again among a crowd of dockers going home. But on the return trip they sat in the shade of the saloon and Lizzie found that they were holding hands, very naturally.

Joe blew out his cheeks. 'I've been given a bit of a thrill three times today. What are the chances of that?'

'Three times? What were they?'

'There was the foaming deep and Young Edmund –'

'Always dramatic . . .'

'There was the engines from Hades.'

'They sucked my breath out. And? You said three thrills.'

'This.' He squeezed her hand. 'Being with you, Lizzie Parsons.'

'Oh, this.' She squeezed his back. 'Joe Gibson.' And so they sat until the ferry docked, and were the last to leave the saloon.

* * *

The Arsenal hooter sounded and Jack Parsons saw his workforce out of the shop. The trays of Lee Enfield cartridges were stacked for collection next to the narrow gauge railway that ran past the building, and the men found their caps to doff them as they passed the superintendent at the door. When the last had gone, Jack went inside and stood at his desk, marking off the day's output. But not too quickly, and only when the cleaner's key turned in the lock did he close the ledger.

Dolly Waters came in, her cap jauntier than ever, showing more blonde curls. 'Evening, Jack.'

'Evening, Dolly. Everything all right?'

'Right as rain.' She came in and left the door open. 'Not in a rush tonight, Mr Superintendent?'

'Not especially.' He went to the door and shut it, turned the key.

'Well I am. Sorry, Jack. I started early. I'm finished after I've done you.' She came over to his desk and opened the ledger, ran a finger down a column of figures. 'I see you can still add up straight.'

'I never drank that much last time.'

'And quite right, too. Does you no good in the end.' She closed the ledger, put a hand into his jacket pocket and pulled out his watch. She looked at it and put it back. 'Home, Jack!' she said. 'Saturday night's Saturday night an' Thursday evening's Thursday evening.

Get home for your tea.'

'I'm not in a great rush tonight.' He turned to look through the open door of the dark cupboard where the fire blankets were rolled. 'I thought I was on a promise . . .'

'Well you're not, Jack, not tonight. I've got to get home to Mum and Dad.'

'Come on, Doll! Put down that broom . . .'

'No, sorry, Jack, nothing doing.'

'It helps keep me sort of steady.'

'And I can't help that. Tonight I'm getting home to time on account of my dad not being too good.' She left Jack's side and started sweeping. 'So if you don't mind, I'll get on with my work.'

Jack shrugged, buttoned his jacket and put on his cap. 'As you wish. But make sure you don't miss the brass shavings under them vices.'

'No, sir.'

He walked out, went to the offices to write a report on Fred Mason, who was using time on Union business, and walked the long way home to Sutcliffe Road with a look on his face to freeze anyone's friendly nod.

He answered the door when Lizzie knocked, standing back in the hallway and folding his arms at her. Behind him she could see her mother looking anxious.

'So what sort of game do you think you're playing,

madam?' He was blocking the way, looking as if he might just push her out of the house again.

'What *game*? No game.' But she felt twisted with guilt; she hadn't come straight from Flo's – that seemed hours ago – and she'd only thought to skew her beret on to her head at the last second. She tried to look puzzled, but she knew that her guilt had won.

'Where've you been, young lady?' He'd never acted the hard father with her before and she felt afraid. He unfolded his arms to slam the door and folded them again, bigger.

'I told you I was going to Flo's after school. You said I could. We had strawberry muffins and ginger beer, and her dad came in and talked and talked and talked. I couldn't get away.'

'She's right. We knew where she was going, Jack . . .'

He spun round at his wife: 'Shut up!' – and came back at Lizzie. 'Is this Flo of yours a Russian toerag with the look of a broomstick on end?'

'No, she isn't; of course she isn't.'

'So who was that Johnny walking with you up past the Woodman?'

Lizzie could only shake her head and look puzzled. 'Eh?' But he wasn't going to move. 'Oh, him. He just happened to be coming the same way and fell in with me.' She was thinking fast. 'He goes to the Ascension.' Church things were always safe. 'He pumps the organ.

He was at the concert you came to when I was the Mary.'

'I think I remember him.' Her mother came a step nearer. She put on a lighter voice. 'He had a way of pumping with one hand behind his back that was very amusing . . .'

Lizzie nodded. 'He's just a boy from around here. Like the fellowship boys at the Mission.' She was surely on safer ground now.

'All holy, holy, eh?' Her father stood closer, and taller. 'Then by what right does the Lord allow a boy from the Ascension to plant a kiss on a girl from the Mission? Permission from Above, is it?'

Oh, no! He had seen that, and she'd been surprised herself at the time. 'It was only a peck on the cheek. Sort of friendly.'

'He'll know sort of friendly when I catch up with him. You're a little madam, young lady. You're a little twicer!' He turned to her mother. 'How can a father let his daughter out of doors if any Tom, Dick or Harry can kiss her in broad daylight on the streets of Plumstead?' He stepped back to look Lizzie up and down. She knew her beret was at a saucy angle, she could feel it on her head like a question mark, and having Joe's arm around her waist had creased her uniform so she didn't look a bit like a Greenfield girl who'd taken afternoon tea at Blackheath.

'He just fell in with me.'

'Name?'

'I don't know.'

'You don't even know this lout's name but he reckoned he could kiss you? You little slut!' He unfolded his arms as if he might hit her.

'*Jack!*'

'Only on the cheek.' Lizzie started crying. 'I'd just had a nice tea . . . and Commander Lewis came in from London . . . and talked about the government and the strikes. He's very high up . . . and I felt special, on the crest of a wave – and I didn't think for a second the boy would dare to kiss me . . .'

'Yes, that's what all the women say when they get into trouble.'

'Jack – the girl can't be blamed if some boy takes a cheeky advantage. Let her through.' Lizzie's back was still only an inch from the front door.

'Don't you go against me, woman.' His voice had a growl in it. 'You be quiet.'

Lizzie's inside was in knots. She'd been so selfish and secretive, setting up situations to suit herself, making use of Flo's invitation and cutting it short so she could meet Joe. The worst thing was, and she was shaking at the thought of it, neither she nor Joe would come out worst – because someone else would.

She was allowed to go to her bedroom to change, and

when she came down she laid the table and tried to eat the meal her mother had made; the start of an evening that went as badly as she knew it would. The supper didn't please her father. 'Suet dumplings served with a bit of bacon? Them's for lamb, woman.' He pushed his plate aside. And he wouldn't go outside for a sit and a smoke despite the evening being warm. Instead he stayed in the kitchen with a newspaper, every twist and shake of it the sign of trouble to come. And her mother's trembling fingers as she couldn't thread her needle made Lizzie want to get out of the house, run to Woolwich and throw herself into the ferry foam. Her father's mood tonight was all her doing – and her mother was going to pay dearly for what she'd done today.

It was the longest night of her life, hearing every sound. She wanted to pull the counterpane over her head and yet she couldn't. Was that a whimper from downstairs or a dog whining in a garden? Had someone slammed a shed door, or was that the table pushed against the door in the kitchen? She wanted to know what was going on, but she didn't. This was her fault, her own selfish fault, and her mother was suffering for it – and she could only imagine what sort of spiteful thing he was doing: something that wouldn't show, something twisty or sharp, man against woman and worse than the black eyes women couldn't hide. She curled and uncurled in the bed, threw back the covers, pulled them over again. She couldn't bear her thoughts. It should be her who was suffering. She Chinese-burned her calves, she pinched her chest and her thighs. She should be the one who was hurting for what she'd done – and as her mouth filled with the taste of hatred she swore to God that she would put this right. What was going on downstairs was criminal, and she would move heaven and earth to bring it to an end. She sat up. She would stop her father's wicked behaviour if it killed her. Yes, if it killed her.

Chapter Eight

Flo wondered how Lizzie's mother was, and Lizzie just stopped herself from saying, 'All right, thanks. Why?' Stupid! Of course, her mother was supposed to have been nauseous the day before, but that had gone out of her head. 'Better, thank you. A little better. I'm so sorry about . . .'

'That's all right. Mama thinks you should have told me and gone straight home from school. She wouldn't have been put out. Papa would have made short work of the muffins. Never mind. Hey ho . . .'

A slight tension with Flo began the longueurs of Lizzie's day when, after that dreadful night, Lizzie was determined to speak to Miss Mitchell. It was as if school didn't want to end; every forty-minute lesson was like an hour and the breaks seemed like half holidays. When the final bell rang Lizzie said a quick goodbye to Flo.

'My apologies to your mother . . .'

'My best to your ma . . .'

And Lizzie made off as if going home; but as soon as Flo was out of sight she doubled back into the school and hurried up the stairs to the staff common room. She did what the notice told her to do: KNOCK ONCE ONLY AND WAIT, and the door was eventually opened by Miss Rogers, the maths mistress.

'Parsons. Yes?'

'Is Miss Mitchell there please, Miss Rogers?'

'Will she want to see you?'

'I don't really know, ma'am.'

Miss Rogers turned and called into the common room: 'Charlotte – Eliza Parsons is asking for you,' immediately shutting the door.

It was quickly reopened. 'Eliza.' Miss Mitchell smiled.

'Miss Mitchell – could I have a word, please?'

From the look on her face Miss Mitchell guessed this wasn't about Rump Parliaments or Oliver Cromwell. 'Come to my classroom.' She took Lizzie up into the history room. 'You look strained and tired. Are you in some sort of trouble?'

Lizzie felt like crying right then, but she held off as Miss Mitchell ushered her to a double desk and sat in another across the aisle.

'Have I been too discreet, Lizzie? I felt it wise for us not to have any contact about the cause for a little while.'

'No, ma'am.'

'*Charlotte*, come on, *Charlotte*, please – unless it's Cromwell's Commonwealth you're here to talk about.'

'No . . . Charlotte . . . it's not school. And it's not the cause.'

'Oh?' Charlotte Mitchell pursed her lips.

'It's . . . it's . . . personal.' Lizzie didn't know how to start; she'd hoped the words would just come out, but all at once this seemed such an awful thing to be doing – telling tales on her father, and such shocking tales at that.

Charlotte Mitchell leant across and patted the back of Lizzie's hand. 'You can tell me whatever you want. Just say it, dear.'

And Lizzie had to; it was that or get up and go home in a state. She took a long look at the desk lid. 'My father is hurting my mother. At night.' It was out. '*Actually* hurting. Doing things to her. Spiteful things, but I don't know what.'

'Oh, my goodness! Physical things? Abusive?'

'Yes.'

'You've seen him?'

'No, but I know it's happening – and my mother won't let it show. He's clever: what he does, it's never on her face or her hands, but I've seen rinsed-out cloths – pink, I think with calamine lotion – and she keeps her sleeves rolled down even doing the wash. And heaven knows what's happening . . . anywhere else.' And now she did cry, at just the suggestion of her mother's suffering. 'And it was me who caused it yesterday. I did something stupid and made my father angry, and my mother stood up for me.' She wiped at her eyes, caught her breath. 'He didn't hurt me, he never has, but I know he hurt her, I know he did. It went quiet and sinister, all unnatural, like some secret ceremony going on downstairs.'

'My goodness! You poor girl . . .'

The tears were rolling, and now the mistress was beside Lizzie in the same desk. She moved her over to put an arm around her and to dab a handkerchief at her cheeks. 'You shouldn't have to suffer this, no more than your mother should.' She held Lizzie until the tears stopped. 'Well, this must not go on, Lizzie. If it's not a black eye or a bruised cheek . . .'

'No, it never shows.'

'A lot of men know they'll get away with a wink and a warning from the police, so they quite proudly let their women wear the marks of their abuse . . .'

'Nothing like that; you wouldn't know.'

'Like a lot of things that go on. But it will take some thinking about, some advice sought, and possibly some action by you.'

'What can I do? Please tell me.'

Charlotte Mitchell kept her arm around her as she

thought, just lowering her voice. 'I think it would help if you could get evidence of the abuse, a significant piece of clothing, perhaps, before it's washed – the pink of calamine could be well-rinsed blood – you know the sort of clothing I mean.'

Lizzie nodded. She did – Charlotte meant undergarments, things her mother might hide in the bottom of the laundry basket for Mondays when the copper was on.

'Items get lost, sometimes, don't they?'

'Yes. I'll do what I can.' Lizzie could see the sense of getting evidence: the police couldn't be expected to take a schoolgirl's word about things without evidence to back it up.

'And I'll arrange for you to meet some WSPU people again – because we're not only suffragists, Lizzie, we're feminists: we won't sit quietly under male injustice.'

'No. Thank you.'

Charlotte took her arm away and stood. 'So head up and face the world, Lizzie Parsons. "*Res Non Verba*".'

'Yes.' Lizzie stood too, tried a smile, and with confirming nods at each other they went together as far as the stairs, where with a pat from Charlotte Mitchell on her cheek Lizzie hurried down and out of the school – crying again the moment she was in the road. It was all too much. The mistress's kindness had done for her, but they were tears of relief, too. She had told someone; the truth was out and she wasn't harbouring a secret any more, despite the worry of the cat being let out of the bag. As she took her familiar route home, the streets somehow seemed as if they belonged in a slightly different land today.

Things were quieter that Friday night, but sometime over the weekend there was that difficult thing she had to do – find evidence of what her father was about. It would hang over her until she had at least tried. Then there would be Sunday, with Mission as usual in the morning and Sunday school in the afternoon, but after that she'd have a big decision to make. Would she dare to meet Joe at the pond? Could she run the risk of her father seeing them again, or somehow finding out? Most summer Sundays he'd be in the garden with his flowers for a bit, before he'd go out for a mooch somewhere or watch a few overs on the common. Which could be dangerous. Well, she'd have to see how the land lay when the time came.

But with all this going on in her head, the tin lid was firmly put on writing a poem.

As luck had it, on the Saturday afternoon her father went out to meet someone from the Arsenal, and she was alone in the house with her mother who was cleaning the parlour grate – a Saturday job on hands and knees that couldn't be left once started.

'Love is a plaintive song,
Sung by a suffering maid,
Telling a tale of wrong,
Telling of hope betrayed . . .'

The singing was from a show they'd seen at the Grand – and all the while it was coming from the parlour, Lizzie knew where her mother was. Now was her chance then! Picking her moment she went to the laundry basket on top of the copper.

'Rendering good for ill,
Smiling at every frown,
Yielding your own self-will,
Laughing your tear drops down . . .'

She reached into the laundry basket. The personal things were always at the bottom beneath the towels, with the sheets and tablecloths on top. She lifted and raked but while there were shirts and camisoles, knickers, stockings and socks there was nothing to be found that was stained pink or worse.

'Never a selfish whim,
Trouble, or pain to stir;
Everything for him,
Nothing at all for her!'

And nothing at all for Lizzie Parsons. There was nothing in here to incriminate anyone. But weren't the words of that song a sort of evidence – a song of sacrifice by a suffering maid? Wasn't that a very telling song for her mother to be singing? Perhaps she could show the song sheet to Charlotte Mitchell – although it wouldn't cut much ice with a magistrate, would it?

'Love that will aye endure,
Though the rewards be few,
That is the love that's pure,
That is the love that's true!'

And was that why Alice Parsons put up with her husband's behaviour? Every verse was telling a story. Did her mother see it as some sort of duty to go on loving a man whatever he did to her?

The singing had stopped, and so did Lizzie's search.

'Oh, my knees! And if I don't get the black off my hands I can't let Mrs Winter in.' Her mother came from the parlour, giving the range a poke to boil a kettle. 'So . . .'

And Lizzie knew what that '*So* . . .' meant. She would need to be private for writing down what Mrs Winter wanted put in her letter.

'I'll make myself scarce, then. What time's she coming?'

Her mother looked at the clock. 'Oh, my goodness, in half an hour.'

'I'll skedaddle then. How long will you be with her?'

'Under the hour, probably. She'll be to the point. Thanks, lamb.'

Taking pencil and paper from her satchel Lizzie left the house and crossed over at the end of her road on to the grass at the top of the ravine. She would write a note to Joe, explain why he couldn't see her the next day, and when she'd got it right there'd be time to slip it under the flowerpot inside his gate – because she had to let him know she just daren't risk meeting him. But how to put it, what to say, that was the problem. The shorter the message the longer the pondering, that's what her mother said. She looked all around her, over at the common, up at the sky, back across the road at the Mission Hall. And, thank you! *The Mission!* She had a brilliant thought. Put something positive in it. Don't make it a 'no' but a possible 'yes'. And a possible 'yes' was *Wednesday Club at the Mission,* which was a young people's club from half past six to eight o'clock – and there were lots of laughs. In the colder weather there'd be draughts or tiddlywink tournaments, or games of skittles or sing-songs. In the summer they'd go out for bat and ball games on the common, or send semaphore messages across the ravine, or play hide-and-seek in the gorse bushes. And the big 'yes' about it was, if people ever had a friend or a cousin visiting they could be taken to Club for the evening, pay a ha'penny for their drink and biscuit and be made welcome by the members Pastor called his 'urban missionaries'. So why not Joe?

Her father wouldn't walk in on them at the Mission, would he? So, yes, yes, yes – why not invite Joe?

She started on her note but lost focus as she thought about the prospect of seeing him on Wednesday. She remembered the feel of his arm around her waist on the ferry, that kiss on her cheek, the way he wasn't so gangly when he was with her, even his hair being content to lie flatter – all of that made her smile. And what a joy it was to have a friend who made her smile inside.

Dear Joe, I can't meet you on Sunday, but can you come to the Club at the Mission Hall, 6.30 on Wednesday? Just as a friend, mind! No pecks on the cheek, thank you! Lizzie x.

It took ten times as long for her to add the kiss at the end as it did to write the rest of the note – but she made sure to keep the 'x' very small. Jumping up, she ran to Rose Cottages to slide it quickly under the flowerpot at number two with a corner showing, and she headed for home, her head full of the Wednesday night to come, hoping like mad Joe would show up. In the middle of everything else going on, she knew it would do her the world of good.

Joe stood in the cottage doorway as his gran sang at him, refusing to let him inside until she'd got to the end.

'Hold your hand out naughty boy

Hold your hand out naughty boy

Last night in the pale moonlight
I saw you, I saw you
With a nice girl in the park
You were strolling full of joy
And you told her you'd never kissed a girl before
Hold your hand out naughty boy.'

'What's all this, Gran? Got a job at the Grand? Or are you chasing off the mice?'

'What's all this indeed?' She pulled something from her apron pocket. 'This bit of paper was minded to blow itself down the road till I dived on it.'

'Oh, yeah?'

'Who's this Lizzie, then? Some little friend you're keeping secret?'

'Give me that!'

'Aha!' Gran put the paper behind her back while they did a jig.

'She's just a friend. She was in the Christmas thing at the church.' He grabbed the note and crunched it into a pocket.

'A bit soft on her, are you?'

'Not especially.'

'Course. "Just a friend".' Gran made to go into the scullery. 'I'd believe you except for the teeny little kiss she's put at the end.' She laughed at him. 'Know you now, don't I?'

Joe stared at her, red and serious in the face. 'Do

you? Me knowing myself, that's the main thing.' And he went upstairs to get out of his shop boy clothes.

Lizzie had to focus and refocus on the teacher's comments at the end of her history essay. Beneath her assessment on her Oliver Cromwell homework, Charlotte Mitchell had written '*8/10. This is better.*' And underneath it was an added message in pencil: '*Saturday afternoon: 130 Hyde Vale, Blackheath. Summer social. 2pm.* C.' Lizzie snapped her book shut like a mousetrap going off.

'What did you get?' Flo was twitching beside her.

'Eight.' Lizzie put the book into her satchel. 'How about you?'

'Six.' Flo pulled her pussy face. 'I do better when history's about kings and treason and tortures.'

'Don't worry. We'll soon be starting on Plague and Fire.'

'Lovely!'

Lizzie turned away from the pigeonholes and headed for the courtyard. 'I'm going outside for a breather.'

'Aren't you hungry?'

'My sandwiches can wait ten minutes.'

'I won't come with you, then. Did you just hear my stomach?'

'I thought it was a horse on the meadow.' Lizzie

gave her a friendly push and went out of the door. She wanted space for herself and some calm, somewhere to get over the surprise of Charlotte Mitchell's invitation. The seat around the robinia tree would be just the place. Friendship was a complicated thing – and she was going off Flo just a bit – but how complicated would friendship with her schoolmistress be?

She stared up at the robinia leaves, no longer bright and cheerful when seen from below but dark against the sky. She looked again at the note written beneath her essay. Against the red ink of her marks, that soft pencil seemed so very personal – and secretive. And what sort of social was being held in Hyde Vale – wherever that was – on Saturday?

So, yes, she decided, *very complicated* was the answer to her Charlotte Mitchell question. But wasn't her life already complicated enough? Dare she add to those complications?

Chapter Nine

Charlotte Mitchell was still in Lizzie's head that Wednesday evening, even as she walked to Club. It was weird, new, to know a schoolmistress outside school. Teachers had always been like people from a different world, as if they didn't do the ordinary things of life such as shopping or travelling on trams and buses. She'd been surprised at Elementary School when Miss Nunn told them she'd been to see Wilkie Bard sing 'She Sells Sea Shells' at the Grand. At the Votes for Women shop Miss Mitchell had seemed more like a teacher on an out-of-school occasion, but after that comforting time in the classroom and that pencilled note in her history book, Miss Mitchell being Charlotte didn't seem so strange – someone she knew who would help get justice for her mother. And the start of that would be at Hyde Vale on Saturday.

'Do you know where Hyde Vale is?' It was almost

the first thing she said to Joe when she saw him – Joe, coming along The Slade all arms and legs and big grin. 'You came then?'

He looked down at himself. 'Seems like it.'

'That's really good. You'll like Club – it's a lot of fun.'

He looked over at the Mission building. 'Where are we, in there?'

Lizzie nodded. 'Thanks for coming. Only, I can't do anything on Saturday evening. I've got to go to Hyde Vale and I don't know when I'll be back.'

They went inside the Hall, Joe taking off his cap and wiping his feet.

'So *do* you know where Hyde Vale is? I've got a meeting with my history teacher.' Which wasn't a lie, was it?

'I certainly do. You might remember my little spill with the paraffin . . .'

'Do I not!'

'Well, I was delivering with Smollett's cart down there one day and the thing ran away from me. Had a mind of its own – and it's quite steep, Hyde Vale.'

'Joe! What was on the cart?'

'Flour for the baker's at the bottom!'

'No!'

'I scooped a lot of it up. Good for brown bread or digestive biscuits . . .'

'You fibber, Joe Gibson!' Which was not the best

moment for Pastor Cassidy to come out of the vestry. 'Oh, this is Joe, Pastor – he goes to the Ascension, pumps their organ, and he's visiting our house, so I invited him to Club.'

The pastor smiled. 'Welcome, Joe, in the name of the Lord.'

'Amen.' Joe wrung his cap.

A few of the others came in through the doorway.

'Who's this, Lizzie?' A few big eyes from the girls.

'A friend of mine – Joe.'

Joe stood to attention, until he wobbled.

'Well, well, well, Lizzie Parsons!'

'We'll have a wide game in the ravine,' the pastor told them –

'Yes!'

'Good-ho!'

'Great fun!'

– which took some of the attention away from the visitor.

Capture the Foe was a favourite, all about two teams with either red or blue PT bands tucked down the backs of their collars. One side chased to grab the others' bands, who sprinted and dodged to keep them safe, running from the top of the ravine over here to the top of the ravine over there. Coming back the chasers and the chased changed over – the winners being the team with more bands intact.

While Pastor Cassidy went ahead Mrs Cassidy picked the teams, and a couple of girls were quite disappointed not to be on Joe's side.

'He looks like a good runner.'

'He could catch me any time!'

Firmly, Lizzie led Joe across the road to the top of the ravine – both of them in the reds, all of whom turned their backs while the blues scattered to hide in the gorse bushes and behind trees.

Pastor Cassidy's whistle blew to set them off. 'Separate!' Joe told Lizzie. 'I think they'll go for me.'

'Big head!' Lizzie ran towards the steps to the pond. And sure enough Joe drew a lot of the blues the other way, giving her a clear climb to the pastor up on the common. Five others got through, too – mainly because Joe was Target Number One, drawing a couple of boys who were definitely out to get him. He zigzagged and doubled back, jumped over gorse and swung round trees, but when Bertie Mackintosh rugby-tackled him he was sat on by a couple of girls and had the breath bounced out of him.

'Your Joe's a good sport, Lizzie – I hope he doesn't mind being squelched.' On the contrary, Lizzie thought he might be quite enjoying it.

Lizzie's side won in the end, but over lemonade and biscuits the girls made such a fuss of Joe – which he let go on – that she couldn't help feeling that she'd lost.

Sipping and munching he told her how to get to Hyde Vale, but they had to say goodbye in front of the others. 'Cheerio, then, Lizzie. I'll see you soon for sure.' He smiled at her, and winked. She smiled back, but that was all; somehow she wasn't in the mood for winking tonight.

Jack Parsons worked on Saturday, mornings until noon, but that didn't mean he'd always be home by half past. Being a supervisor he would wear his 'half day togs' which he said made him feel easier about going for a pint with a mate at the Woolwich Infant, or dropping in for a game of darts at the Woodman. Alice would do a bit of shopping and Lizzie would be free to meet some of her friends. So going to Miss Mitchell's social at Hyde Vale was no great difficulty for her. But she didn't make a big thing of it.

'Mum, Vera says there's a band on Bostall Heath, we might pop down there this afternoon.' Which brought just a nod and a smile. But she had to look her best, so she chose a pretty dress and found her summer boater in the top of her wardrobe – skipping quickly out of the house when Alice went to the shops.

She took a bus from Plumstead Common to the top end of Greenwich Park and walked on from there. Joe's directions had been very good – but all the way her mind had been filled not with him but with thoughts about where she was going, whom the others would be, and how she was going to fit in with them. She hadn't done badly among strangers at the Catford shop, but everyone had been busy and she'd had a job to do. The talk had been gloves not generalities, while a social would be a different kettle of fish. If this one was like the Temperance socials on the common it would be all sports and glasses of fizz, a raffle, perhaps a speech, lots of mingling and having to talk to people about all sorts of things. Oh, dear! But what was making her nervous above all else was the special person she was going to meet. Which person would she be? Miss Mitchell out of school, or Charlotte Mitchell hugging her in her desk? Everything taken together, this was a dilemma of a day, and Lizzie wouldn't have surprised herself if she'd turned back at the top of Hyde Vale and gone straight home.

There was no sign of either person when she knocked at number 130. A maid showed her past a few people in the hall, through the drawing room and out to a terrace and the garden, which sloped upwards to a large beech tree at its top. It hadn't been a good summer for weather and the sky today was mostly cloud, but the garden was filled with young women wearing summer blouses and light skirts held by tight belts, talking and laughing in small groups. Lizzie had heard them from the house, sounding not unlike breaktime at Greenfield High, but this seemed more like a party than a Votes for Women gathering – and most of the women here were younger than the Catford people. A couple of the younger mistresses from the school were there, who smiled and seemed to make no bones about Lizzie being 'a girl', asking how she'd got there as she looked about for Miss Mitchell, and her stomach really twisted when she came out of the house. She looked so beautiful with her eyes sparkling and her hair full and free.

'Lizzie! You came – I'm so pleased your parents said yes.'

'My mother did. And she said my father would, too, if he'd been at home.'

Miss Mitchell put her head close to Lizzie. 'You will remember, won't you, that I'm Charlotte, not Miss Mitchell?' – as she linked arms and took her to meet the women up and down the garden.

'This is my friend Lizzie from Plumstead. It's her first time, but she's all for the cause.' *Her friend!* Lizzie consciously had to close her mouth.

'Hello, Lizzie. Do you like elderberry cordial . . .?' She was offered a glass.

Another told her, 'Plumstead? My uncle belongs to the bowls club on Plumstead Common . . .'

And, 'We need determination, Lizzie – and may I say you have very determined eyes . . .' This young woman was wearing a purple and green necktie.

A third clapped Lizzie's arms heartily. 'What jollier way to spend a Saturday afternoon!'

The air was light as the voices rose up the garden and into the beech branches, some of the conversation small talk and funny, some of it serious and political. And Lizzie could see why she'd been invited. She heard the words 'submission' and 'demean' as often as she heard the word 'vote', her spirits lifting with a feeling of support as she thought how appalled these women would be at what her father did to her mother. She felt in very good company here.

'You like the look of our little lot, Lizzie?'

'I do, I surely do.' And she knew to whom she was speaking. *Charlotte.* Oh, definitely *Charlotte.*

'Then I have a proposal to put to you.' Charlotte took her aside and lowered her voice. 'Quite shortly Will Crooks – he's the Woolwich Member of Parliament – will be holding a Labour Party meeting in the Seamen's Mission Hall and we want to put pressure on him to give us more support. Really, the way the national Labour Party behaves sometimes it's almost like they're in league with the Liberals. His men will be sitting targets for our leaflets and we need them to ginger things up. What do you think? Would you like to come on a peaceful protest with us?'

Lizzie wanted to say yes. Everything about today

said she *had* to say yes. Although . . . 'It would depend on the when and the where. My father isn't easy over my comings and goings. But I'll certainly come if I can.'

'Splendid. I couldn't ask for more.' Charlotte brushed a fallen leaf off Lizzie's shoulder. 'That's greatly pleasing.'

They were standing on a small step halfway up the slope, chatter and laughter all around, listening here, joining in there – when the garden fell into a sudden hush. Everyone's eyes were turning to the terrace beside the house where a late arrival had come through the French windows, an older woman wearing a long grey coat and a wide-brimmed hat sashed with purple, white and green.

'Mrs Crayfourd! How lovely to see you.'

'Ruth! I'm so pleased you're out.'

The young women in the garden hurried down to greet her.

'How are you?'

'Are you eating better now?'

The woman smiled. 'I am, since I'm eating the way God intended.' Her voice was husky.

Charlotte's cheek touched Lizzie's. 'Ruth Crayfourd. Heroine of force feeding. Holloway Prison.'

'But it's very good to be among friends outside.' Mrs Crayfourd's voice was controlled. 'Please excuse my throat.'

The maid brought her a cup of tea and she was offered a seat at a small table. Everyone crowded the terrace, leaning and squatting, Lizzie and Charlotte with them. Up close Lizzie could see the decoration Mrs Crayfourd was wearing, its ribbon in the suffragette colours and the medal inscribed 'Force Feeding'. *Force feeding!* Lizzie had only ever been tempted into eating anything.

'I fear they've damaged my throat with their pipes and their funnels . . .' Mrs Crayfourd sipped, and it seemed to hurt. 'But only pro tem, I hope.'

There were murmurs of the same hope. 'Can you bear to tell us about it? Or would you rather forget?'

'Forget? I can never forget, we mustn't forget, so I'll tell you what happens if you can bear to hear it. Everyone should know what they do to us, and be prepared for it.' There wasn't a rustle to be heard in the garden. 'I won't go into the general conditions, you can imagine them – degradation, being treated as common criminals and not as political prisoners, plank beds, cold cells, coarse underwear if at all, odd-sized shoes, and being known by a number and not a name.' Her voice had a cultured accent that didn't match these images. 'But if you refuse to eat, prefer to starve than live under their thumb, they use their bullying strength.' The afternoon had darkened and the mood changed. Mrs Crayfourd, a practised public speaker, straightened her back and looked around at them all.

'They send the women warders into the cell first so you're less likely to throw things at them. But the men aren't far behind, to hold you down while they force your head back and push a hard rubber tube into a nostril. But my nostrils are narrow, and push as they might they couldn't get it in; as answer to which they used a steel gag to clamp my jaws open and screwed it wide enough to force the tube down my throat . . .'

There were moans of sympathy, and tears on many of the faces.

'I retched and bled – but believe it or not I was one of the lucky ones. Those who for one reason or another weren't fed by nose or mouth had tubes thrust into their rectums, and you can imagine the pain of that . . .'

Faces twisted into that pain, eyes shut against it.

'. . . Even so, we must not lose this fight! For those still suffering in prison, for the sufferers to come, and for every woman who needs to be treated as an equal human being, we have to win the day!' Mrs Crayfourd stood up and took in a deep breath. 'A movement is only as good as its members, my friends.' Her voice was suddenly stronger, like a singer breathing from the diaphragm rather than the throat. 'Each individual person has to live and act for the cause in their own way, and with the whole of their heart.' She paused and looked around at the nodding heads. 'And the way I have chosen, friends, says we have to take more forceful action. Leaflets are not enough.' She snapped her fingers. 'Soapboxes and platforms are inadequate. We have to fight their force with our force – hurl more stones, fire more pillar boxes, attack more targets!' She opened her arms wide. 'Res Non Verba! We must go forth, sisters, and we must win!'

There were cheers and a burst of clapping, although not from everyone. The garden had become a very different place. Mrs Crayfourd's speech seemed to have both inspired and divided it. But she hadn't finished.

'Remember this. You can be imprisoned as a pacifist as well as a militant. Either way, suffragist or suffragette, your principles can still lead to degradation and force feeding – so I say,' – a long pause – 'go for it! Go for it with open eyes and with women's courage!' She clenched her fist, pumped it, stood still for a moment – then turned and walked into the house.

Lizzie's heart was thumping. She glanced sideways at Charlotte, who was looking towards the house with her lips parted. As the clapping died she turned to her. 'Much to think about, Lizzie, dear.'

'Yes.' Had Charlotte said that for her benefit, not to influence her one way or the other? Or could it be that Charlotte had true doubts over which course to take? Either way, Lizzie felt in her heart that she would want to do *something*.

A couple of Greenfield mistresses came to talk to Charlotte and she was drawn away; after which the afternoon petered out, certainly for Lizzie, and with farewell handshakes and pecks on cheeks people began leaving. After a goodbye squeeze on the arm from Charlotte – 'I'm so happy that you came, Lizzie' – Lizzie left for home, too, feeling lifted in many ways: about the women's movement; about her mother, where she could see some hope in this female solidarity; and about her friend, Charlotte, with whom she would always want to act for the cause.

She had planned to have another go at her poem the next day. Jotting down those random ideas the other night had brought a ray of hope, and after the hope of Hyde Vale a theme began to stir her thoughts. Her father had gone out before Sunday school and wouldn't be at home to put her off with stupid suggestions – so yes, she'd take out her exercise book and have another go.

But she didn't get home to start it yet, because walking home from taking her Sunday school class, who did she see leaning on the railing at the top of the ravine steps, looking at her from under the peak of his cap? Joe Gibson. He crossed over. 'Hello, Lizzie Parsons. Might I ask – do you fancy a walk up the Red Road?'

That stopped her. 'Why, what's up there?' He was the way he'd been on the ferry, smiling, standing as still as he could, looking into her eyes without a blink. Club night on Wednesday just blew away and she smiled back at him.

'There's no blackberries yet. But there's not your dad, either. I saw him coming out of the Old Mill and he walked off Woolwich way, pulling at his watch chain.'

Lizzie thought about it. The poem could wait for an hour, her mother would think she'd gone for a walk with the girls so why not a walk with Joe Gibson instead? While the sun was shining . . .? 'I can't be long. But don't we have to go past your place? What if your gran's looking out?'

'Which she might be, she likes a good nose up and down the road. So what?' He doffed his cap and crammed most of his hair under it again. 'Let her see what a treat you are.'

What was that? Her, a *treat*? But she could see he'd meant it as a compliment, and in his embarrassment he'd turned his face away and was taking gangly steps along the pavement. The Red Road was like a country lane with a view over the river; a walk up there with Joe would be very nice.

'Only an hour at the outside. I've got to get back before my father.'

'I haven't got a watch myself, I sold it to the man who winds up the sundials in Greenwich Park.'

'I'll know when. I'll start feeling jittery.'

They walked past Rose Cottages without a twitch of lace curtain and started along the red clay lane, once more holding hands.

'I haven't got a dad to worry about, Lizzie. My mum died when I was born. He went off into the army and never came back.' Joe raised his cap in a sort of 'goodbye and good riddance' salute.

'So you don't know how they got on?'

'How do you mean?'

'Together. Rubbed along. Your mum and dad, before she died.'

He looked puzzled. 'No, I never knew either of them. What about yours?'

Lizzie looked at the ground. Had she expected this, is that why she'd asked her question? So, what should she tell him? She had to say something. 'Well, my dad's . . . sort of . . .'

'Sort of what?'

'He's . . . well, sometimes he's a bit . . . rough . . . with my mum.' There. She seemed to have known she would tell him.

Joe had stopped, but she dropped his hand and walked on, thinking hard. Should she say what went on, what she suspected? Did she want to let that much out?

He caught up with her. 'He's one of that sort, eh? A bit handy?'

She looked at the awkward way Joe stood, thought of his hair always fighting his cap, at his face always showing the way he felt, this Joe Gibson who had no side, no secrets, no pretence – and she knew she had to trust him.

'He hurts her. When I'm in bed. Nasty things, I don't know what he does, but it's private stuff. I know he does, but I can't prove it. When he's in a mood, when something's gone wrong, when she's crossed him over something . . . she has to pay for it. She always pays.' It was out. 'And although I want to stop it, Joe, I don't know how.'

Joe stood square on to her, taking a step back. 'Lizzie! How terrible! Poor you – and your poor mum!' He took off his cap and put it on again. 'But you know what? No one should have to put up with the bullies of this world – the factory bullies, the men with a bit of power like Smollett, and the men who rule the roost behind closed doors. Bullies have got to be beaten, Lizzie, they've got to be stopped. We have to take action, tell the world, do whatever works.' He was waving his arms enough to take off. Then all at once he was still and his voice went quiet. 'Is your mum a bit like you?' The question took her by surprise.

'How do you mean?'

'Just that, really. Are you a bit like your mum . . . generally?'

Well, how did she answer that? She looked up and around her, at a puffy cloud, at the green blackberries, at a caterpillar on a nettle. 'I suppose in lots of ways I am, certainly a lot more than I'm like him. I've got her eyes and her hands, we both like singing and writing, lots of things he doesn't.' But there was a bigger difference, too, wasn't there? Her mother was gentle. 'I'll tell you what, though . . .'

'What?' He'd never been so still since she'd met him.

'. . . I would never let the spiteful things he does to her be done to me, not by anyone, ever. I would never keep my mouth shut for the sake of the street or the church or my children.' Her eyes began to well up. 'A person would have to finish me off before I suffered anything like that . . .'

'Lizzie!' He faced her, holding both her arms. 'I'll protect you. I'll never let any bad things happen to you. Run straight up to me, day or night, bash on our door, we'll take you in – and your mum if she wants. And I'll make the biggest fuss about it that anyone ever heard, all over Plumstead and Woolwich.' He eased her towards him, held his cheek against hers. 'You'd be protected – and loved, I can tell you. I'd never let a single bad thing ever happen to you.' And he kissed her, a surprise touch of lips at first, then more pressing. She somehow kept her balance and she kissed him back – until his cap fell off, and their laughter marked the time to go.

Now the poem started to come to life. The talk at Hyde Vale had given her an idea for a theme, and that kiss had made her feel bright enough to tackle anything. She sat in the garden and turned to the back of her exercise book, where some of her notes began to make more sense than others, and as she read and jotted a few words a pattern gradually seemed to emerge. More than that, when she wrote a first line the words took on a rhythm, which led to a second line, and almost of itself a sketchy verse began to come. She read it over. Writing a poem, it struck her, was like solving a puzzle you'd set yourself.

'What're you up to, young lady? I'll want a bit of deckchair space if you don't mind.' Her father was standing on the edge of the grass, his feet apart like a sailor on a rough deck.

'My poem.' She closed her book and kept a firm hold on it.

'Oh. Very good. Wise school, choosing a clever girl to write their poetery for them.'

He couldn't say the word properly, but his Sunday drink in Woolwich with whoever it was had at least left him with a smile on his face. He took another deckchair from the shed and set it back on its lowest notch. 'Wake me up when tea's ready.' But his snorts and grunts soon sent Lizzie into the parlour, just to keep herself focused on her poem. She felt lifted by the way it was coming, and when the time came for laying the table she had an outline with two or three rough verses. And it didn't stop there. By bedtime she'd done some polishing; the thing really had a shape, and with everything peaceful in the parlour she went upstairs to stretch out under her sheet feeling good, lying there knowing why that was. She was pleased with her start on the poem, but more than that she could still feel the press of that kiss with Joe – which told her more about things than any words could manage.

Chapter Ten

It was a typical Monday morning in Smollett's shop. Joe spread fresh sawdust around the paraffin drum and gave the shop floor a good sweep. He put that morning's delivery of eggs at the bottom of the stack and cut sugar paper into squares for making cones. But the first customer through the door hadn't come for eggs or for sugar. As Cyril Smollett was still doing up his apron, Ena Collins, a shrivelled little shrimp of a thing, pushed at the door and edged towards the counter.

Smollett looked as if he was minded to set the cat on her. 'You again? Where's your mother? Not come home yet, I should think.'

Ena looked puzzled – and scared. She half-smoothed a scrap of paper from her pocket and put it on the counter. Smollett used a little finger to straighten it. 'Lard, on tick?' he boomed. 'She wants lard on the slate? Well, you can tell your mother her slate's full, my girl. Over-full. Ready to crack!' He said the word itself like the crack of a whip, and Ena Collins's small body shivered. 'A bit less on booze and more on housekeeping and she could *pay* for her lard. So you tell your mother the answer's no. Go and get a handout from the Poor Board.' Smollett loomed over the counter like a giant over a hilltop. 'Got it?'

But, small as she was, Ena didn't budge.

'Mr Smollett . . .' Joe took a step towards the shopkeeper – who ignored him.

'Go on, child!' Smollett wrote 'NO' on the scrap of paper and threw it at Ena. 'Get home and tell your worthless Irish mother she's getting nothing here till she pays off some of her debts.'

Ena shook her head, distressed. 'I daresn't, mister.'

Smollett came round the counter and stood over the child, thrusting his face inches from hers. 'Your father needs to take a stick to that feckless woman. A stick! Good and hard!' He grabbed his yard rule from the counter and brought it down with a sound like a shot from a gun. 'A lesson she won't forget.' He brought the rule down again, closer to Ena, and louder. 'Now get out!'

Ena was crying now. She had wet herself and was standing in a puddle of fear. She looked up at Smollett and kicked at his shin, running out of the shop and into the road, almost under a tram.

Joe chased after her but she'd run down an alley and was soon out of sight. When he went back into the shop Smollett was rubbing his shin, wrinkling his nose at the puddle in front of the counter.

'Get a cloth to that,' he commanded Joe. 'The filthy little urchin!'

But Joe was folding his arms, not calmly but with a twitch. 'Get a cloth to it yourself. You made her do it. You clean it up.' His voice was high and strained.

'*What?*'

'You need your nose rubbing in it. You're a big bully, Mr Smollett, and a disgrace to decent people. You frightened her half to death. Ena Collins can't help what her mother is.' He took off his apron and threw it into Ena's puddle of pee. 'You're a bully and a cheat and a fiddler and it'll be good not having to watch you at it. I feel sick being in the same shop as you.'

Smollett puffed and blew. Joe walked to the shop door and held it open for an artillery officer's wife coming in. 'Don't set him off,' he told her, 'that great bully's just made a little girl wet her drawers.' He walked off down the road towards Woolwich: no jacket, no cap – but with a very satisfied look on his face.

Not just a man of words.

After a peaceful evening with her mother, Lizzie went

to sleep feeling pleased with herself. Since she'd last worked on her poem some of its creases seemed to have ironed themselves out and there was a strong line running through the stanzas. Charlotte's newspapers, her afternoon at Hyde Vale, and the situation at home had all given her something she wanted to say, and as she'd read over the fair-copied piece it dawned on her that she hadn't been writing this for the school or the competition at all – but for herself. It was *her* poem.

All the same, she hoped Miss Abrahams liked it, her '*Res Et Verba*'.

She felt less confident next day in English, and was quite fluttery by the end of the lesson. 'I'll catch you up, Flo.'

'Don't hurry, it's only housecraft. What a waste of time – there are girls to do all that sort of thing.'

When the classroom was empty Lizzie took out the fair copy of her poem and gave it to Miss Abrahams, who said 'Ah!' and immediately read it through, holding it up before her as if about to sing it. Suddenly the room felt airless. Miss Abrahams's eyes gave nothing away, they rarely did. Was she pleased? Would she tear it up? Had Lizzie disappointed her? Was the mistress sorry to have asked Eliza Parsons to write a poem for the Westminster Central Hall? Her Varsity gown told the world how clever she was, so was this effort just ignorant rubbish, something flimsy and pretentious, not worth the ink used for writing it out?

'Thank you, Eliza.' The English mistress folded the paper and put it on her desk. Lizzie stood waiting for a moment – Miss Abrahams was a lover of long pauses. But nothing followed; it was, 'Now, off to your next lesson.'

'Yes, ma'am,' Lizzie left the room and hurried to housecraft. So had '*Res Et Verba*' been graded before it even touched the desk? With her heart racing in her chest one moment and up in her throat the next, the uncomfortable feeling of not knowing the poem's fate lasted Lizzie through the rest of the day.

'Are you ill?' Flo asked at break.

'I'm fine. Just a bit shivery, which is jolly weird when it's so warm . . .'

'As long as you're all right. Did it come on in English? Is that why you stayed behind?'

'Not particularly.' But in spite of the cock of her head, Flo was getting nothing out of Lizzie about '*Res Et Verba*'; not yet, anyway – because it was probably rubbish. 'Come on, Flo. French next, then it's home.'

'*Ad-mi-rable*. I'm *prêt* for some *patisserie sur le balcon*.'

'*Bien sûr*.'

What a straightforward life Flo Lewis had.

* * *

But it wasn't home for Lizzie – not straight after school. Someone who should have been hard at work in Smollett's shop was lurking behind a tree at the end of the private road.

'Erk! There's that paraffin boy!' Flo wrinkled up her Duchess nose. 'What does he want?'

'*I* don't know.' And Lizzie truly didn't. 'Anyway, I'm off home. See you tomorrow, Flo.' She walked as far as she dared then looked around, and thank goodness Flo had gone. She went back towards Joe, who was in his best cap and a crisp new collar; Sunday clothes, not weekday.

'Joe – what are you like that for? Where've you been?'

'I've had an interview this afternoon.'

'An interview? Where?'

'In the Arsenal.'

'*The Arsenal?*'

'You know, that big place down by the river that makes guns and stuff.'

'Very funny. Why?' What was he on about?

'Because I told Smollett his fortune this morning and he gave me the sack.'

'Joe!'

'He had it coming to him. He was a really rotten bully to a little girl . . .' And he told Lizzie about Ena Collins.

'Oh, Joe. So what happened with you at the Arsenal? You went for a job?'

'Yup.' He looked very pleased with himself.

'And?'

'I hit the right time. They're building up their railway rolling stock and taking on more people to run it . . .'

'What's rolling stock?'

'Engines and trucks. There's a railway in the Arsenal . . .'

'I know.' Lizzie's father talked about it sometimes. It ran on small rails and sometimes trucks came off. 'That's dangerous, isn't it?'

'Not as dangerous as explosives. Anyway, they're giving me a trial in the sheds, only greasing stuff and cleaning carriages, putting oil in the lamps, nothing marvellous to start with. But I'll be working Arsenal hours, forty-eight, not Smollett's sixty or seventy.'

Lizzie put her hands on her hips. 'Well I never.'

'I'm not a Trade Lad – you have to go back to school for that – but a proper hand. You can call me George if you like.'

'George?'

'George Stephenson. A man of the iron road.' He folded his arms and stood there proudly.

'I'll call you barmy. You could be jumping out of the frying pan and into the fire. You don't know what bullies there might be in your sheds. They're everywhere in this life.'

'Agreed, but they'll be bullying me, not little girls and old ladies.' He swivelled his cap around, peak at the back, put up his fists and shadow-boxed. 'Just let 'em try.'

'Oh, Joe . . .' Lizzie started walking for home. 'When do you start?'

'Next Monday. Eight till five and every other Saturday morning.' They walked together holding hands.

'What's your gran going to say? She got you the Smollett job, didn't she?'

'She'll say something horrible about him. She only ever worked for him to pay off her rent. He owns half Plumstead, that man.'

Lizzie squeezed Joe's hand. 'I'm just thinking. You were a shop *boy* for Smollett, now you're going to be a railway *man*.'

'Earning more money, too. I'll be able to put a bit by. But I'm still the same Joe Gibson. Me, inside, I'm not going to change, Lizzie . . .'

'And don't, Joe, because I like you the way you are.'

'That's good to hear.' But his face had turned very red.

They dropped hands in Garland Road, smiled at each other, fixed to meet at the pond on Sunday and went their different ways, Lizzie heading for Sutcliffe Road with Miss Abrahams and '*Res Et Verba*' forgotten; because, what next for Joe, standing up for what he believed to be right, changing his job to do something totally different? And wobbly railway trains were a lot more dangerous than any Mr Smollett. She just hoped Joe could keep his long arms and legs well out of harm's way, that was all.

Lizzie had no idea it was coming. The start of the lesson was just like all the others. Everyone filed into the English room and sat in their usual places, opened their grammar books and sat up ready for Miss Abrahams to open hers. No one spoke, it wasn't allowed. They were waiting for the lesson to start abruptly with the opening lines of a novel they hadn't read, or a description of a book character. 'I wonder how much you'd enjoy having a sister like Mrs Joe Gargery to bring you up "by hand"?' – which would hook them into the lesson. Miss Abrahams was no Charlotte Mitchell, but no one slept in English. Today, though, she really sat Lizzie up.

'Today we congratulate Eliza Parsons.' It came from nowhere, confounding Lizzie. Everyone swivelled and Flo made a noise in her nose. 'A few chosen girls were invited to submit poems for reading aloud at the League of British Girls' Schools' annual general meeting in Westminster. One of the submissions was

Eliza's –' she managed a smile at Lizzie '– and it is her poem that has been chosen by Miss Tudor Hart and myself as the one to go forward into the final thirty. Well done, Eliza!' Miss Abrahams led a polite round of applause. She nodded at Lizzie. 'More anon.' And that was that; they were on to *Great Expectations* in no time at all, to which Lizzie paid more attention than she'd ever done before.

'You didn't say.' Flo looked pleased for Lizzie and disappointed at the same time, one of her specialities. 'You secret old thing.'

'I was told it was to be confidential.'

'*Very* confidential, not to tell a good friend.'

'Miss Abrahams forbad me. I had no choice.'

'What's it about, anyway, or is that confidential, too?'

'I'm very sorry, Flo, but it is, for now.'

'I wonder why she asked you?'

There was no answer to that so Lizzie shrugged, but she found they were sitting just a little further apart in history, and that certainly didn't change when Charlotte Mitchell asked Eliza Parsons to stay behind at the end of the lesson.

'Two things,' she said, when the classroom door was closed. 'You might think I've been very quiet about your problem at home, Lizzie . . .'

'No, not at all.' And Lizzie truly didn't. Things

were in her own hands for a while, trying to find that evidence.

'. . . But I've been thinking deeply about it. Let's sit down.' Charlotte led her to a desk at the front of the room, sitting with her side by side this time and not across the aisle. 'Have you heard of psychiatry?'

Lizzie had. She remembered her father reading out something from the *Daily Mirror* – about a mute girl who had been cured by a psychiatrist. 'Waste of money. Women are best seen and not heard,' he'd said.

'It's German, isn't it?'

'Austrian. By Sigmund Freud. Well –' Charlotte turned to her, and now she seemed to be someone new: not the teacher nor the suffragette friend but more like the older sister, saying what came next as if she knew Lizzie wouldn't want to hear it, but had to. 'There's a word for what your father's doing. It's called sadism, a sexual disorder of spite.' She said it in a very matter-of-fact voice, like Lizzie's mother with a tricky subject. 'And the partner can welcome it or not.'

'Not! Not! She must hate it!' God! The thought of her mother welcoming her father hurting her! The thought of that was even worse than what he did to her.

'I'm sure. But no more details – except that sadism doesn't always have to be sexual, the desire to hurt can be triggered by many things: jealousy, discontent, plain straightforward anger.' Lizzie sat still. That sounded more like her father. 'It might be one thing one day and another thing another. But Lizzie, I want you to know this, and it's very important.' She moved closer, their arms and knees touching. 'My father has a psychiatrist friend who runs an outpatient clinic for these sorts of problems. Dr Rayner, at St Thomas's Hospital in London. It could be arranged for your father to see him, and I'm sure my father would help with that.' She lifted one of Lizzie's clenched hands from the desktop, opened out her palm and laid her own palm on top of it, a warm feeling of calm and comfort. 'Be reassured that help can be obtained if a person is willing.' A new sort of glow spread inside Lizzie, which lasted until Charlotte took her hand away.

'On Wednesday this week there's a Labour Party meeting at the Seamen's Mission Hall. I told you about it. Do you think you can come?' Charlotte was being the suffragette again.

'I'll try.' After what Charlotte had just been saying this talk of Votes for Women came out of the blue, sooner than Lizzie had expected. But Wednesday was a good night where her father was concerned. When she went to Club he went to some sort of Arsenal social with Wally Waters and never got home before she'd gone to bed. 'I think it'll be all right.'

'We want to spread ourselves around the gallery

for when we drop the leaflets. Lots of supporters are going to be at an Emily Wilding Davison meeting in Lewisham, so we'll be short of numbers.'

'I'll let you know tomorrow.'

'I'd be obliged. Thank you, Lizzie.' Lizzie wondered that she hadn't called her Eliza; she had suddenly sounded so formal.

But thank goodness, Flo hadn't waited outside the classroom. Perhaps she thought her friend was being altogether too favoured by the staff. And like anyone in that position, Lizzie's was a very awkward place to be in these days.

On the other hand, Lizzie's good news made getting approval for her Wednesday evening assignment fairly easy. As soon as they were sitting up to tea she told her parents that Miss Abrahams had announced the winner of the school poetry competition in her English class. She puffed out her cheeks in imitation of the teacher's pudgy face and she put on her deep voice, which made her father laugh and her mother frown – until she got to the point.

'"Today we congratulate Eliza Parsons": so I won, out of everyone!'

'My girl the winner! Out of all the girls at Greenfield High School!' Her father threw down his fork, stood up and patted her head.

'Not *all* the girls, just the ones she asked.'

'That's the same thing. And what a credit to us.' Her father saluted her mother, tucked in his shirt and sat down again. 'Our Sutcliffe Road girl goes to Greenfield High School and beats their best – and there's a few snooties and smarties up there, I know.'

'That's very rewarding, Lizzie.' Her mother leant across the table and patted her hand, the smile on her face a reward in itself. 'Your hard work there is certainly paying off. Now what's next, I wonder?'

'I suppose Miss Abrahams sends the poem to the Girls' School League. The big wigs have to choose which one's going to be recited.'

'But achievement enough already, lamb. The Lord Jesus be praised!'

'It was a foregone conclusion, woman. Our girl was always going to win, hands down. So let's hear it, Lizzie, this poem. Won't give me indigestion, will it?'

'No, it won't, because I haven't got it. Miss Abrahams kept it, and my exercise book's in school.'

'Oh. Another time, then.'

'But I did wonder if I could go to school on Wednesday evening . . .' Lizzie kept her voice light and normal. 'The Sixth Form are doing the dress rehearsal of their end-of-term play, and they want an audience.' This was certainly the time to ask.

'And what play's that? Not *Charley's Aunt* – that's a

laugh and a half. I'll come with you if it is.'

'No, it's *The Critic,* a Restoration piece.'

'All about furniture?'

'It's Sheridan, Jack.'

'Like I said!' But he caught his wife's warning eye. 'Only joking.'

By now Lizzie knew she was all right. Her father was in a merry mood, and his permission was clinched when she lied that at the end of the evening Flo's father would walk her home to the top of their road.

'That all seems very sound and proper.'

'Enjoying Sheridan, and doing your own writing. You're a true lover of the English word, Lizzie.' Her mother said it with such pride – and Lizzie felt awful. Lying to her father was no problem at all, but lying to her mother twisted her up inside. But it was all in a good cause, wasn't it? Votes for women, if they got them, would be bound to help the cause of Alice Parsons and others like her, so being a support to Charlotte could only be to her mother's good.

Chapter Eleven

Joe Gibson wasn't a Trade Lad and he wasn't an apprentice, just a young Arsenal hand working on the railway. It would be a long time before he got on to a footplate other than to sweep it out, and meanwhile there were mundane jobs he had to do, which took a bit of skill. Filling a locomotive lamp with oil to just the right level needed a steady hand, and trimming its wick had to be timely or it would smoke up the glass, illuminate nothing and take a lot of cleaning. Old Gummy Griffin was his charge-hand, but a slight problem was Gummy having no teeth, his talk coming out in pops and puffs and his thin old cheeks sucking and blowing like frail bellows – although with a little imagination Joe managed.

That afternoon's work was cleaning the passenger rolling stock. 'Geff your broomf, boy.' *Pop, pop, pop.* 'Sheff six. Swophing ouft the knifeboofs.'

The railway carriages housed in shed six took workers from the Arsenal gates to the different workshops and stores all over the site, and then back again at the end of the day. Just like trams and buses, the back-to-back wooden seats were separated by tall boards, easing the discomfort of overcrowding. These seats and their carriages were called 'knifeboards'. Now, at the tail end of the dinner break, Gummy and Joe were heading for shed six to sweep them out ready for the evening runs.

A narrow-gauge track led into the shed and fanned out into four lines of carriages, but otherwise the job had nothing to do with railways. It was just cleaning up other people's mess.

'Yoof starf offer end.' *Pop, pop.* Gummy waved into the darkened distance. 'I'll staff thiff'n.' *Pop and blow.*

'Right you are, mate, I'll go down there. You save your legs for dancing the Lancers.' Joe shouldered his broom and headed for the far end of the shed. This job was a matter of opening a carriage door, sweeping both sides of the knifeboard on to the floor and into the metal pan he'd set on the outside step. And it could be a rotten task. One seat of a knifeboard couldn't be seen from the other side, and after the carriages were shunted into the shed they became good places for private meetings between Arsenal men and cleaners and army officers' domestic servants. But today when

Joe put the pan on to the step of the furthest carriage he stepped back in disgust. The place was never pleasant with what people left behind, but today someone had emptied their bowels in a violent way and Joe almost brought up his dinner.

He fetched water and the oldest broom he could find – and got on with what he was paid to do, but as the carriages started being marshalled for the evening runs he found old Gummy lying along a knifeboard seat and woke him up. 'Here, Gummy, how long have you been doing this job?'

Gummy sat up and blew in and out. 'Couldnff say.' Joe told him what he'd had to clear up that day. 'Geff it now an whenff.' He looked surprised that Joe had even mentioned it.

'Well next time I'll come and get you to give me a bit of a hand.' Gummy didn't look put out by that. 'Or I'll let the carriage run around the site for all the world to see.' And he went off towards another knifeboard with a stench still in his nostrils.

The Seamen's Mission Hall was a popular public meeting place for all sorts of events. Lizzie and her parents had been there to see *The Mikado,* and schools sometimes held their prize-givings there. It was a large building, converted from a Baptist tabernacle, with rows of seats downstairs and a gallery on three sides above. It was where Will Crooks held election hustings and this was his venue for Wednesday's Labour Party meeting. Crooks was an entertaining speaker, and his weekly meetings in the Market Square always drew good crowds – and he would that Wednesday evening, no doubt.

Lizzie didn't wear her school uniform. 'It's an evening event,' she told her parents, 'Flo isn't wearing hers.' So as not to stand out she put on her everyday beret, a quiet blouse and a dark skirt, but she made sure to pinch her cheeks and try to look as pretty as she could. And she was very pleased that she had when she saw who was walking along Beresford Street. It was Joe Gibson!

'Joe!'

'Lizzie! What are you doing here?' He waved an arm at the Union members who were congregating. Lizzie looked around. Charlotte and the others hadn't arrived yet; it was all men who were drifting into the Hall.

'I'll tell you when I see you, Joe. But I'm meeting some of those Hyde Vale people from before.' She put a finger to her lips and nodded a hint of a secret. Joe seemed to twig and said nothing. 'But what are you doing here?' Was he going into the meeting? He'd be a Union man for sure, but whether he was Labour Party would be another matter.

'I've walked along with Gummy, he's a member. I'm off home for my tea.' He was with an older man who nodded.

Lizzie looked around again. There was still no sign of Charlotte.

The older man said goodbye in words she couldn't catch, and she hoped Joe would go quickly. But he was standing there as still as ever he could. ''Fore I go, I've got something to ask you. It's right at the top of my mind today.' He was still Joe Gibson, he would always be Joe Gibson; cap askew, arms like semaphores and feet that thought the pavement was red hot.

'What is it? Can't it wait?' Lizzie didn't want Charlotte to see him with her; for now she wanted to keep her worlds apart.

'Course it can wait. It's just I've had a bit of an idea about my job – but it's nothing big, and nothing soon. It'll keep very well till I see you at the pond on Sunday.'

'Yes. I'll see you on Sunday, hear about it then.' *Go, Joe. Please go now, dear, dear Joe.* It took some effort for Lizzie not to look around again for any sign of Charlotte.

'Yup. I'm off for my tea. See what surprise Gran's got on the cheese shelf.' And there outside the Seamen's Hall he gave her a kiss on the cheek and with a wobbly wave he skipped off over the road.

'Aye-aye!' A Labour man stood to attention.

'Me next, girl!' And another.

Lizzie tried to compose herself for Charlotte again, stood there waiting the way she'd been before. And here she was, with two of the younger women Lizzie had seen at Hyde Vale, all three crossing the road with confident steps and their heads held high.

'Lizzie! Lovely to see you. Thank you for coming.' She waved towards the others and introduced them. 'Belle and Roberta. You know them, don't you?'

Lizzie hardly did, but they had met and been friendly at Hyde Vale.

'Now, Lizzie, I shall introduce you as one of my pupils, together with Belle and Roberta.' Both could pass as senior girls.

'Those were the days!' said Belle.

'So it's "ma'am" tonight. I'm your history mistress and I've brought the three of you along to see democracy at work. We shan't get in otherwise.'

More of the Labour Party men of Woolwich were arriving, and the vestibule of the hall was crowded as Charlotte took them inside and sought out a steward.

'I did enquire earlier and I was told it was all right. I'm from Greenfield High School for Girls, these are my history students, and they're studying the political scene. I was told we might observe the meeting from the gallery.'

'Who told you that?' The steward frowned at her.

'Mr Crooks's office said we'd be welcome. He's all for –'

'Not the membership secretary?'

'No, I was in touch with Mr Crooks's office.'

The steward looked around him, the general jostle growing. 'Mr Crooks and his party are up behind the platform. I can't leave here to check.' He looked the small group up and down, and none of them was dressed in purple or green. 'You've got no bags, nothing I need to search?'

'The girls have brought their brains along, that's sufficient.'

He stood thinking. A crowd of boisterous men were waiting to get in off the pavement. 'Very well, then – but no noise up there!'

'We'll be as quiet as mice.' Charlotte looked at all her girls very sternly.

'Mum's the word, ma'am.'

The steward pointed them to the gallery stairs, but as Charlotte led them up another woman suddenly came pushing in from the street.

'I'm with these people,' she said, pointing at Charlotte and following on. She had her arm in a sling. 'I'm late after a nasty fall on an uneven pavement.'

The steward was besieged by men showing him membership cards, so he waved the woman in. Perhaps from her accent he thought she was the headmistress. But as they reached the gallery Lizzie realised who had just joined them. It was Mrs Crayfourd, the militant suffragette who had spoken in the garden at Hyde Vale.

'I do wish she hadn't come.' Charlotte reached into the pocket of her skirt and drew out a pack of pamphlets. She gave some to Lizzie and pointed to a central spot on the left side of the gallery. 'Watch for my signal. We'll all throw together.'

'I shall go as near as I can to the platform.' Mrs Crayfourd edged along to a seat at the front of the gallery and took some pamphlets from her sling.

They were alone up there, downstairs crowded and noisy, and Lizzie's insides turned as the hall began to quieten. It was like the dimming of the lights at the Grand, with expectation in the air. 'Order! Order! Best of order, please!' Her heart beat faster. This was it; she was in here, and whatever happened she was part of things. She hadn't dwelt on what might happen to her, but the chairman's voice had rung out like the Lord High Executioner and Charlotte had lied to get them in. Would throwing leaflets be taken in good part? Was Charlotte right and they'd only be ejected? Would nothing else happen to them?

Charlotte must have seen the look on her face. 'Don't worry, Lizzie. They won't want any fuss. They'll want the press to write up the meeting, not give space to us.'

Lizzie crept to her place and sat low in her seat, while the platform party came on to cheers and claps – and there was no doubt which one of them was Will

Crooks. He was a burly, bearded man standing in front of a Union banner and clutching the lapels of his jacket. He let the applause swell and swell and then he raised his arms for quiet. Lizzie was drawn to him with the rest, but she was keeping an eye on Charlotte for the signal to throw her pamphlets down.

'Brethren, fellow members, we have many people to be grateful for, not least our loving wives who have let us out tonight. And we give thanks for ourselves, for the growing strength of our party – because if anyone were to doubt how strong we are, they should see the huge assembly here. I'm sure our friends from the press will record this "house-full" commitment to the cause of the Labour Party.' He waved down to the press table at the front. The hall clapped as a couple of reporters from the local papers scribbled away. Even up here Lizzie felt the unity in the hall, but nervous now with the thought of it being turned upon her.

'Together we are strong. Together we stand for workers' rights in a sense of brotherhood. And remember this, and tell it to your Liberal mates in your shop, in your yard, on your building site: a worker who seeks to gain advantage at the expense of his workmates is like the man who stole a wreath from his neighbour's grave and used it to win at a flower show.' They laughed and gave him a round of applause. 'The Labour Party is an army of one!' There was a cheer to that. 'United we bargain – divided we beg.' Another cheer, louder. He linked arms with the other men on the platform, and stepped to its edge, a rehearsed move. 'Arm in arm, working men are stronger together!' This had the hall on its feet.

Which was the moment. Charlotte, Mrs Crayfourd and the others were standing, too – and just as Will Crooks spotted them Charlotte shouted, 'Votes for Women!' and scattered her leaflets over the balcony. The others scattered theirs and now Lizzie suddenly found her courage. She shouted, 'Equality for the female!' and threw hers, too.

Amidst angry shouts from below, the gallery doors burst open. But not before Mrs Crayfourd had ruined the demonstration. She took something from the sling around her neck and set a match to it, throwing it at the platform: a small canister that hit the stage, broke open, and billowed thick black smoke all around it.

'What have you done for the Cause?' she called in her stronger voice. 'Mr Crooks, you support a government that tortures women!'

Lizzie was grabbed by a steward and pulled to the stairs, scared she'd be pushed down them. A policeman in the doorway blew his whistle into the street and ran back inside. But the stomach-dropping sight came from the side door to the platform as two stewards carried out an old man who was struggling to breathe.

It was the party chairman who had called the meeting to order.

'Get an ambulance! He's sucked in a lung-full!'

A friend was by his side. 'He's got a dicky chest. He needs oxygen, fast!'

'Now see what you've done!'

'Murder, this is!'

The chairman was laid on a bench, heaving and gasping for air. Will Crooks was with him, wiping black powder from the man's face and hands.

'You'll pay for this. The Union's on your side, but you've no right doing this!'

The vestibule and the hall inside had gone very quiet. Two more constables came running in, one of them sent straight off again for an ambulance and the other for a van from the police station; and all the while Lizzie and the others were held in fierce grips, forced to watch the chairman's struggles for breath.

Will Crooks looked into Mrs Crayfourd's eyes. 'This could be murder!'

'It was protest smoke, that's all, stage stuff, relatively harmless I should have thought.' Mrs Crayfourd looked defiant. 'No one can prove intention to harm.'

'It's not for you to say,' a policeman told her. 'The magistrates will decide on the crime.'

'The judge, more like.' Will Crooks looked genuinely angry. 'If old Walter dies you'll hang for it, madam.'

Hang? Lizzie felt frozen. The 'gingering' act of throwing leaflets had turned into a nightmare. And Mrs Crayfourd was standing there looking as if she had no fear of being hanged as a martyr.

An ambulance soon drew up outside, the chairman still fighting for breath as he was carried out to it. It was quickly followed by a police van, the sort Lizzie's mother would point out to her in the street and give her a slight thrill. Now she was pushed into this one, bundled into the back with dire instructions not to talk. But the looks of Charlotte and the others said everything that needed saying to Mrs Crayfourd. She had invited herself into their peaceful demonstration and changed their fates from being thrown into the street to being thrown into prison, and possibly worse. Lizzie was numb. It seemed like all this was happening to somebody else. Right now, in the back of this bumpy van, it was as if she didn't know a boy called Joe Gibson, she hadn't written a winning poem and she didn't live in Sutcliffe Road with her mother and father. She was heading for Holloway Prison, and possibly the gallows. Since seven o'clock that evening she had stopped being Eliza Parsons and become a militant suffragette, ready to be a number instead of a name, and having to face whatever prison dished out to her. And in that unreal state she stared ahead as she was driven through the streets of Woolwich to the police station, in the grip of the strong arm of the law.

With the others she was arraigned by a desk sergeant and spattered with insults by the constables. Some looked ready to give more than insults: their grips had shown their strength, and in pushing the women through the doorways they had pressed hard on the backs of their heads to bend them double. Slaps, punches and kicks would be no surprise in this hard-knock place. The surprise was Charlotte, twisting herself face-into-face with the constable who was holding her. 'Touch me like that again and I'll report you to the Home Office.' She pointed to his collar. 'Constable 211RW. I've got your number.'

The constable leered at her. 'You can have a slap to add to your complaint if you don't shut your mouth.' He looked at her as if he would give her one, too, and none of his colleagues seemed ready to intervene.

But Charlotte only stood taller. Lizzie admired her brave expression, especially her eyes with that steel in them. 'And I've something else to say.' Constable 211RW put his hand into the leather loop on his truncheon and drew it up six inches. She didn't flinch, but went on, 'You will not dominate me!' Her voice was throaty and strong. 'I am a grown woman. The others are grown women except Eliza who is a schoolgirl, taken by surprise at the turn of events. I invited her to join us and, whatever any others might have done, I take responsibility for her. She came simply to spread our literature.'

It had no effect, except that she wasn't slapped and no one gripped her again. 'It's not for you to accept or deny responsibility.' The desk sergeant rattled his pen in his inkpot. 'The girl was present at the act and was part of it, and will be charged with the rest of you with common assault and possibly with manslaughter or murder.' He looked down at Lizzie's entry. 'Still under seventeen, just, so they may not hang her, at least. Be grateful for that, and be quiet.' He took a bunch of keys from a board on the wall, placed it on the counter and told the constables to take the offenders down to the cells.

She wouldn't hang! That was a huge relief – but still Lizzie was this demonstrating suffragette about to be locked up for breaking the law. And the down-to-earth reality of it hit home when she was pushed into a cell and the door slammed shut. The place was cold and smelly, with white glazed-brick walls, a bare wooden bed, a chair, a slop pail, a high barred window and a metal door with a hatch in it. She stood and waited, heard doors clanging, and after a short while came the sound of Mrs Crayfourd singing in a level, defiant voice.

'Raise the song of liberation!

Rouse the fire in every heart!
For the weal of all the nation
Women claim their equal part!'

With a great rattle of keys and a clang the cell door suddenly swung open and a female warder came in. No nonsense. 'Undress,' she commanded. 'Everything.'

Lizzie stared at her, a cold stone of a woman, and looked at the cell door, which had been left wide open. She saw a policeman pass.

'Will you shut the door, please?'

'No. Do as you're told.' The wardress threw a garment on to the bed. 'Else the men will force you.'

Helpless. Degraded. A nobody. This was the same as Mrs Crayfourd had described. And would it get worse? She did as she was told, turned her back to the door and undressed, putting her clothes on the chair. She shivered. Now what would happen? The wardress went through her clothes, found a Votes for Women leaflet caught up in her vest and put it into her pocket. And that was it. She walked around Lizzie, didn't touch her. 'Put that shift on.'

The grey garment was crumpled but clean. There were no shoes, no stockings, no underwear. The wardress went out, clanged the door shut and locked it. A gas mantel in a ceiling cage popped dimly. Lizzie looked at the bare boards of the bed. There was no bolster, no blanket, no mattress; and in that state she sat there and shivered. But she wasn't numb any more, she was coming back to her own reality. With the undressing she had become Lizzie Parsons again, lonely and frightened, who had been so stupid, been led into serious lawbreaking that could lead to all the horrors Mrs Crayfourd had described.

She put her head in her hands. If only tonight's lie had been the truth and she was sitting in the school hall laughing with Flo at a Restoration comedy.

If only . . .

If only lots of things . . .

Chapter Twelve

Jack Parsons opened the door, a proud look on his face to welcome his clever Greenfield High daughter back from her evening at the play. But it was a police constable standing there.

'Mr Parsons? John Alfred Parsons?'

'Yes.' Jack looked beyond him; there was no one else, no Lizzie, no friend's father.

'Can I come in?'

Jack frowned and stood aside. Alice had come to the doorway from the kitchen. 'What is it, Jack?'

The constable was inside. Alice opened the parlour door. 'Better come in here, please.'

They went in, all standing.

'You've got a daughter, Eliza Ellen Parsons?'

'Is she all right?'

Jack put an arm across Alice. 'I'll do the talking.'

'Your daughter's all right, missus. She's at

Woolwich Police Station charged at the moment with common assault.'

'*Woolwich Police Station?*'

'*Charged with what?*'

'Common assault. So far. But I've got to tell you it could end up far worse.'

'What the hell are you talking about?' Jack Parsons' voice rattled the carriage clock. 'She's at her school to see a play.'

'No, she's not – and hasn't been. She was at the Seamen's Mission Hall in Woolwich where projectiles were thrown from the gallery by the Votes for Women brigade.' The constable looked particularly at Alice, who was standing upright like a suffragist herself. 'There's been a serious injury to the party chairman, and your daughter is among those charged.'

'Our daughter? You've got the wrong person. Must be someone giving her name. She's at Greenfield High School for Girls tonight, watching the dress rehearsal of a play . . .' Alice turned to Jack. 'Isn't she?'

'And she's being seen home by a commander at the Admiralty, how's that? There's got to be a stupid mistake. She'll be here in a minute, I thought you was her just now. You've got a mix-up on your hands, mate.'

The constable shifted his helmet under his arm and brought out his notebook. 'Date of birth, twenty-third of January 1897, address ninety-four Sutcliffe Road, scholar at Greenfield High School for Girls. I saw her give the details to the desk sergeant. Dark-haired girl in an apricot blouse.'

'Oh, my Lord! Who else was there? Florence Lewis?'

'That I can't divulge. They'll all be up in court tomorrow.'

'Not her school friend Florence Lewis?'

'No other child was present, I can tell you that.' The constable closed his notebook.

Jack Parsons swore, profanely and foul-mouthed. 'The little twicer! She's up to some game!' He rounded on his wife. 'You don't keep eye enough on that little madam, I tell you! Being kissed by boys and getting up to God knows what else. You're too bloody lenient by half!'

Alice suddenly crumpled on to a chair and put a handkerchief to her face.

'You can see her at Woolwich Police Station at nine o'clock tomorrow morning prior to court. Whether you'll be allowed to bring her home or not will depend on the charges and the beak.'

'Constable – she's not hurt, injured?'

'Nothing like that, missus. But she'll be sorry and lonely, that's for certain.'

'Oh, dear Lord! Dear Lord Jesus!'

The constable went to the front door and Jack

Parsons ushered him out. 'Nine o'clock tomorrow. I'll be there. On the dot.' He turned back into the passage, muttering under his breath, and walked into the parlour.

'Jack . . .!'

'Don't you "Jack" me. My God, you've got a hell of a lot to answer for, woman . . .'

Lizzie couldn't sleep. She could never sleep away from home, and the police cell was a harsh, sitting-up place. They'd thrown her a blanket and given her a piece of bread and a mug of water; she'd made use of the pail and tried to lie down, but the cell was too cold and noisy: doors clanged, a male prisoner shouted the odds until he suddenly went quiet and Mrs Crayfourd sang her Holloway songs until she finally tired, and the night was filled with the sounds of boots in the corridor and the shutting of door-hatches.

Lizzie's mind went over everything: how trying to help her mother had got her here; how the leaflet-dropping at the Seamen's Mission had been ruined by the militant Mrs Crayfourd; how everything might change for the worse by the state of the choking man. But really churning her insides was the thought of her father going mad when they told him where she was – and how her mother would suffer for it.

Then came the voice, calling along the cells'

corridor. It was loud, it was firm and had no fear in it. It was Charlotte's. 'Are you all right, Lizzie? Don't be demoralised. We are in the right!' It was a welcome voice to hear, and it sounded nearby.

Lizzie went to her cell door and called through the half-closed aperture. 'I'm all right. Are you?' She daren't call her Charlotte, not in here.

'I'm not defeated, Lizzie dear.'

The rap of a truncheon on the cell door made Lizzie jump. 'Shut up and go to sleep.' It was a rough male voice. She heard the truncheon rapping further along. 'And you! Keep your girls' chat for the Holloway yard.'

Lizzie was wide awake now. She pictured Charlotte in a cell like this, lying on a similar bunk wearing the same sort of shift, her hair let down and her mouth set in the defiance she'd shown to the constable upstairs; a thought that brought again the cold fear of what could happen if that old man died. In a well of self-pity she started to cry, quietly in case Charlotte should hear, but deeply and at length. Her tears were fuller and hotter than she'd ever felt them, like every grief she'd ever known running together down her cheeks. They ran and ran until she began to hiccup and at last she had cried herself out. With her throat lumped up she lay on her side on the bunk, closed her swollen eyes and eventually fell into a sleep without dreams, a cold oblivion . . .

Suddenly she was shaken roughly and ripped

from sleep. Daylight was leaking in through the high window and the wardress was standing over her. 'Take that thing off and get your clothes on.' She had brought them with her. 'You can splash your face when you empty your slop.'

Obediently, Lizzie dressed – although denied her shoes – and was taken along the corridor to the wash-place. No one else was there; the other cell doors were shut and only Mrs Crayfourd could be heard, chanting over and over, 'We are not common criminals. We will not eat your food. We are not common criminals. We will not eat your food.' Lizzie emptied her pail down a drain, was told to rinse it out under the cold tap and to wash her hands and face.

'Now half-fill your slop.' Lizzie did as she was told. 'Take hold of a mop.' Several smelly mops were leaning against the wall. 'And a cloth.' These were like cardboard, pegged on a line. 'Now get along –' and she was marched back to her cell – 'you can give this floor a proper clean, and I'll be back when you've dried it off.' The door was shut, the hatch left open, and Lizzie did the best she could to clean and dry the floor. It took a long while until at last she was sitting on the bunk, wiggling her toes to dry them. And after what seemed an age of comings and goings in the corridor, the wardress came back with a mug of tea and a small brown loaf.

'That's to last you the day, if they bring you back here from court.'

It shocked Lizzie. She hadn't properly realised – she knew it but she hadn't accepted it – that this was only the start of her imprisonment. Being given her own clothes didn't mean she might soon go home; there would be the awfulness of standing up in court, being brought up from the cells and taken down again, and then where else would she go – to a real prison? And she was hit again with the terrible thought that if the old man had died she could be held to blame for it with the others – and locked up for a very long time.

She sat and wept again, cried out loudly, her chest heaving as she bent to stop her tears with the hem of her frock.

Bang! The door opened. The wardress came in. 'Look at the state of your face!' She threw her shoes at her. 'Get these on and come with me.'

Lizzie tried to be quick, but she fumbled with her shoes and had to walk from the cell with one foot in and one foot out. She was led up the cell stairs and into the vestibule where the sergeant lifted the hinged end of his desk and took her through to a side room. To be faced with her father, who was standing there with folded arms and a look to kill.

'You cunning little vixen! What game's this? Eh? What game's this?' He pushed at the table between them as if to get at her.

'Steady, Jack.' Like a lot of Woolwich people the desk sergeant would know the medal-winning hero of the Arsenal fire. 'She's a girl who's been led, and if you sit yourself down I'll tell you what's what.'

Still staring at Lizzie her father scuffed a chair round to sit at the table, as straight as a judge. The sergeant sat, too, but Lizzie was left to stand – and finally get her right foot into her shoe.

'I've got signed and witnessed statements from the adult female prisoners. A Miss Charlotte Mitchell – a mistress at your daughter's school – has signed a document to say that your daughter was told that her attendance at the Seamen's Hall was for the express purpose of observing the meeting . . .'

Lizzie daren't look at her father. She was finding it hard to breathe.

'. . . She would have had no idea that there would be a demonstration and so took no part in it, and on the word of this responsible adult we're not putting her up to appear at court. She'll be given over into your custody on the condition of her good conduct.'

Lizzie breathed again. Thank God! And that wardress must have said nothing about the pamphlet she'd found in her vest. But her father hardly looked mollified. His face had that biding-his-time look of a bad night to come for someone. But who would that be? Lizzie had never had him look at her like this. Would she be safer here in the police station tonight?

'So you take her home, and tomorrow get her into her school uniform and take her up to Greenfield School. I've spoke to the headmistress on the telephone.' He paused, significantly. 'But whether or not she'll take the girl back I can't say.'

'Right.' Jack Parsons stood up, knocked over his chair and stood it on its feet again. 'Thank you, guv'nor.' He pulled on his cap and waved an arm at Lizzie. 'Outside.'

The sergeant held the door open and followed them into the vestibule. 'You're a very lucky young lady with a good friend.' He gave Lizzie a knowing nod and saw them into the street.

Not a word was said all the way to Sutcliffe Road. Jack Parsons strode ahead and looked neither to left nor right, up to Woolwich Common, along to The Slade and home. With the flourish of a jailer he took out his keys and opened the front door.

'Inside.'

Lizzie went in, scared he was going to hit her as soon as the door was shut – and with no sign of her mother to defend her.

'Alice!' he shouted into the house. 'Alice Parsons, where are you, woman?'

'Up here, Jack. Making the bed.' Alice came down. Her face was drawn, her eyes puffy. 'Oh, thank you, Lord!' She ran to Lizzie. 'My dear girl!' She gave her a kiss on both cheeks. 'You're home, lamb! You're safe! Dear Lizzy!'

'Mum! Mum! I'm sorry! I'm so sorry. It was all spoilt. It wasn't what I thought. Honestly, I didn't mean to –'

Jack Parsons snarled. 'Listen to her! She "didn't mean to"! She didn't mean to do a lot of things. She didn't mean to tell me a pack of lies to get to do what she did. She didn't mean to make me look like a common criminal, up before the police. She didn't mean to get herself thrown out of Greenfield High School by getting tricked and twisted by a teacher.' He suddenly punched the wall. 'She didn't mean to spend a night in the clink and lose her father's good name in the Arsenal.' He stared at his wife, pulled himself above her. 'Them's some of the things your daughter didn't mean to do!'

'Jack, she's only a child . . .'

'I'll give her "child". She's a clever little chancer, that's what she is. Went with a load of know-it-all suffragettes to break up a meeting and shout their filth at the men of Woolwich and throw smoke bombs at a Member of Parliament. They sent a man to the infirmary who might never come out again . . .'

'Jack . . .'

'All over what? Over what?' His face was crimson and he spat as he spoke. 'Over wanting votes for people who need to keep their place! Get the vote? Get the birch, that's what they deserve, and this clever little madam along of 'em!'

'Please, Jack . . .'

Lizzie hadn't eaten, the hallway was hot, everything echoed, her head was light, she felt as if she might lift into the air – and she was suddenly filled with a weird sense of wildness. Almost in a trance she jostled her mother out of the way and pulled herself up to stand facing her father – staring into his face with her eyes blazing. 'You just don't understand, do you? You're in your own world – because you're all right!' she told him. 'You're one of the privileged few! You're a man and you run a house! You're different and you're lucky.' In her own hallway she was Charlotte, standing up to that policeman. 'So *you* can vote, but what about all the others just as good as you who can't.' Her father was looking at her as if she'd gone mad. 'Better than you, some of them! But they can never put a cross on a ballot paper because they aren't doing jobs like yours.'

'Lizzie, please, leave it, lamb . . .'

'You're first class, they're second class, and we females are third class. That's how you think.' She said it with disgust. But was she really saying this to him? She'd never stood up to him before – and now that frightened her because he didn't like it and he was making room to give her a slap for her cheek. But she was undeterred. 'The unfairness of it! The arrogance of it – that you think you're a better creature on this earth than Mum!'

Somehow that kept his hands by his sides and he turned on his wife. 'I blame you, woman!' He pointed at her. 'You're the fount of these wild ideas. You and your namby-pamby softness, too trusting, letting this little madam go off the rails till we're nursing a viper in our bosoms.' And now it came out into the open, turning Lizzie cold. 'You'll pay for it, woman! You'll pay for it, mark my words.' He stared at her, held his threatening look for a long time. 'You . . . will . . . pay . . . for . . . this!' He swung back at Lizzie. 'And you, upstairs, up to your bed and in it. I'll decide what's to happen to you when I've got your mad talk out of my head.' They were jammed tight in the hallway – until he pushed through to the scullery. 'I'm going to the privy but don't get no ideas! In your bed, you!' He slammed out to the back. Lizzie's mother pulled a face and gave her a do-as-he-says look, then kissed her on the forehead and stood waiting until she'd gone up the stairs and into her bedroom.

The bed was still made from the day before and it looked like luxury to Lizzie after that bare bunk in the cell. She shut the door and changed into her nightie. It wasn't midday yet and it seemed unreal – the bright daylight and being ready for bed when she wasn't ill – but she was the lucky one. Downstairs was her mother – accused of being a kind, soft and loving person, who had awful things done to her by that . . . *sadist* . . . of a husband. Lizzie sat on the bed and dropped her head. And that was only part of the awfulness going on. Charlotte and the others would be up in court soon – and if the old man had died their fate didn't bear imagining: whoever threw the smoke bomb, their crime would be murder, and the four of them would be hanged. And even if the man lived, they'd go to Holloway Prison for serious assault, which was something to shut from her mind – Charlotte with her lovely hair cropped off, rough cell clothes next to her skin, and having those terrible force-feeding things done to her. It was all too horrible.

She looked at her dirty feet. She'd only been allowed to splash her face and hands that morning and then she'd had to mop and dry the cell floor, hot work in a dank place. If only she could get the smell of the police station off her skin. But there was a knock on her door, and no wardress coming in but her mother carrying a bowl of hot water and a flannel. Two minds with the same thought. 'Have a go over with this, Lizzie. He can't object to that.' Her mother put the bowl on the washstand. 'Give me your clothes for the basket and when he's changed and gone to work, I'll bring you up a bite to eat.' Her voice was hushed and nervous.

He was outside, they were alone, so was now the time to talk about what went on in this house? Her mother had just called her father 'he' and not 'your father', and that was a difference today – so could she use it? But with family modesty, her mother went quickly out of the room while she washed, and the moment had gone. So she used the flannel and the luxury of hot water, put on her nightie again, and a short while after the slam of the front door her mother came with a cup of tea and two slices of buttered toast, jerking her head downstairs. 'Your father says I'm not to coddle you. So read your school books and try to drop off – I don't suppose you had a wink last night.' It was loving but straight, the household boat not being rocked, and what cast Lizzie further down was her saying 'your father' again. For goodness' sake! Couldn't her mother see she'd got to find some way out of this terrible state of affairs – because no one else was going to do it for her. And with that thought came the dread that things were going to get so much worse from now on . . .

Chapter Thirteen

Lizzie did sleep for a while but she was wide awake when her father got in from work. So would he come up? And what would happen if he did?

But he came nowhere near her. Her mother brought up cold cuts and a dish of custard and left her to eat her tea in her solitary confinement. When she'd finished Lizzie checked that her school uniform was smart enough for meeting Miss Tudor Hart the next day, then she tried to read and couldn't, so she just lay there listening. She heard the ring of a tradesman's bell, boys playing Rough Riders in the street, neighbours talking in the gardens, her father's voice and long silences downstairs. What she didn't hear was the front door opening or shutting – her father wasn't going out tonight – but eventually there came what she was dreading: the sound of a sinister quiet, the same thick silence as those other bad nights. What was he doing to her? Her thoughts were horrific.

She almost longed for the police cell again because no atmosphere could be as bad as this. She wanted to hear Mrs Crayfourd singing along the corridor and the sounds of shouting and boots and slamming doors, because they had been about justice being done – while what was going on downstairs was a violent crime against a fellow human being. And Lizzie Parsons had to stop it. She'd got to go downstairs and confront her father. She'd got to threaten to tell Miss Tudor Hart, who was a magistrate as well as a headmistress, and ask her mother to roll back her cuffs and show her arms. She'd got to ask her about the other places where she was hurt. And she'd got to have the front door ajar ready to run next door to the Farmers. That's what she'd got to do. Should she wear slippers or shoes, put on her clothes or a dressing gown, carry her hockey stick?

She let out a long, silent sigh. But did she dare – and what would come of it if she did? With the threat of Miss Tudor Hart he would just pull her out of school, send her out to work, carry on ruling the roost and doing his spiteful things, the way he always had.

But these were excuses. The awful truth of it was, she was too scared even to go downstairs and ask for a glass of water, which might have stopped something for a while. When it came to it she was too scared that he'd turn on her and hurt her, too.

She turned this way, she turned that, and in despair

she stuffed soap into her ears and lay on her bed in a shiver of sweat, truly wishing to die.

At the lowest ebb of her life.

She felt just as bad the next day. Her father said her mother had a migraine and was to be left in bed undisturbed. Lizzie could get their breakfast, then they'd be off to Greenfield High and leave poor Mum in peace. So he ate, she nibbled, and with terse commands he strode them up to the school, Lizzie trailing behind, still hating herself for her cowardice. Her mum had to be in a very bad way not to wish her luck on a big morning like this.

Edith Tudor Hart was no elderly headmistress, severe and distant. Her hair might be pinned up in an academic bun but enthusiastic wisps always escaped, which were brushed aside like objections. She was not much older than Charlotte Mitchell and years younger than Miss Abrahams, living for learning, convinced that education was everybody's right. When Lizzie had passed the scholarship examination she had given her a hug and some special words of encouragement. 'Make us proud of you, Eliza Parsons, make Greenfield proud.'

'Better than a cane across the backside, which is all I ever got.' Jack Parsons had been impressed by Miss Tudor Hart. And today he was as obedient as a Greenfield student. The headmistress insisted that he should sit down and so should Lizzie, so they sat like studio portraits on her visitors' chairs.

'Well now, Eliza. What have I to say to you?' The headmistress picked up a sheet of paper and put it down again without referring to it. Lizzie stared at the carpet, not even trying to reply. 'It's a sad story, Mr Parsons.'

'It was her teacher did wrong –' Jack Parsons half rose but sat again. 'She usurped her influence.'

'Miss Mitchell and the other ladies have been taken to Holloway Prison, but you'll be pleased to hear they are not facing capital charges. The gentleman who inhaled the smoke is recovering and is not likely to die. Nevertheless, the crime was very serious. The use of a smoke canister lifted the leaflet-dropping to a much higher level of criminality . . .'

The old man was all right! Lizzie looked at Miss Tudor Hart through a haze of tears.

'. . . But Miss Mitchell spoke up for Eliza both at the police station and in court, and she expressed her remorse at involving a student in a political act.'

'So she'll be sacked?' Jack Parsons leaned off his chair. 'Leading my daughter astray with those peculiar females? She shouldn't be allowed within a hundred miles of young girls.'

Lizzie looked at him. For a few seconds he'd left his mouth hanging open like a man ready for a fight – and Miss Tudor Hart must have seen it. And Lizzie realised that this was the best chance she'd ever have of bringing his violence into the open; Miss Tudor Hart had just had a glimpse of that side of him. The thought welled up inside her like a huge dare again, and she nearly took it; she very nearly did.

'The women's movement, Mr Parsons, has the support of many reasonable people, but what happened on Wednesday evening shows a major division within the WSPU. Many are suffragists, peaceful speakers and leafleteers, but the militants continually steal the newspaper space, which is of course why they carry out their dangerous acts. But their activities should not detract from woman's right to be part of a democracy. That is a cause for many of us.' A good response – but Miss Tudor Hart had jumped in on Lizzie's father too quickly and Lizzie's moment had passed. 'As to Eliza, I apologise on behalf of the school that she has had this experience.' She looked at Lizzie, withholding a smile, then suddenly giving it. 'We're very proud of you, Eliza; your poem for the Trust's annual meeting has gone forward to a panel that will judge between yours and entries from all over the country. And I have to tell you that we have high hopes of it. It's very thoughtful.'

'Yes, miss, she's done well. I'm very proud of my daughter.'

'As is *Mrs* Parsons, I'm sure.'

'Not half she is.' He smiled and nodded like a loving husband, and hatred screamed in Lizzie's head.

'So Eliza shall keep her place here, and she may stay for the day today; we'll ask the boarding wing to give her something to eat at dinner time.' Miss Tudor Hart stood, followed by Lizzie and her father – who tried to have the last word.

'I want that woman punished. She's caused a big rift back at home . . .'

'Whatever the governors of Greenfield High decide to do about Miss Mitchell, Mr Parsons, believe me, she is already being severely punished by the justice system.' And that was it. Miss Tudor Hart crossed the room and opened the door for them. 'Did you bring your books, Eliza?'

'No, ma'am. I didn't begin to hope . . .'

'Then get by as best you can. You're resourceful enough – and we shall look forward to a proper start after the weekend.'

Lizzie nodded, her father insisting on staying to shake hands with the headmistress, and by the time the door was closed Lizzie was halfway down the stairs and on her way to history. She had seen all she wanted of that man for a very long time.

She went nervously into the history room, and found two different people there: the mistress, of course – Miss Evans, one of the women who'd been at Hyde Vale that other Saturday – and Flo Lewis, who today was sitting next to Millie Foster. The rest of the class turned their heads as Lizzie found a desk but Flo and Millie Foster angled their backs away. Without a lot of fuss Miss Evans slipped her own textbook in front of Lizzie, gave her paper and a pencil, and with hardly a pause went on with her discourse on the 'Threat from France'. But not much was learned by anybody that morning. The class and the whole school were abuzz with what had happened to Miss Mitchell and there were some red eyes there in the history room. But not Flo's. The lesson ended with her going out arm in arm with Millie, and Lizzie overhearing very clearly, 'how stupid some mistresses could be.' But if Lizzie were honest with herself, ever since the tea at Ashenden House she had known how Flo took Commander Lewis's line on suffragettes; how close she was to her father, the daughter of a government man who was set against giving women the vote. But the Meadows' fresh air at dinner time dismissed all that from Lizzie's mind. The Lewis's lives could never be of much interest when a cruelty in the Parsons' family had left another member so badly injured that she couldn't get out of bed – and that reality cut deeply into Lizzie's heart.

Her father was indoors when she got home from school, still wearing the best shirt he'd worn that morning, which meant he hadn't been to work. In fact, he had been to Dr Marr's with her mother; and there she was in the parlour with a bandage on her left arm. Lizzie saw with concern that whatever her father had done had needed more than a cuff to cover it.

'That blessed tin-opener, slipped out of my hand as I gripped the handle.' Her mother winced as she raised her elbow. 'Cut me up my arm.'

'Oh, Mum!' Lizzie crouched by her armchair and kissed her. 'You poor thing.'

'It's a little more content now.'

Lizzie's father hardly blinked, as if he was monitoring everything his wife said. And Lizzie didn't believe a word of the tale, anyway. Her mother opened cans of baked beans at the time she needed them, not earlier in the day. No, that bandage covered what the man had done last night – with a fairy tale for the doctor.

'So you can help about the house, my girl. Do the sweeping and the washing-up, then your homework. Get today's tea and go to The Slade for Sunday's dinner tomorrow – straight there and back. I'm keeping a close eye on you, mi'lady, and you're walking the straight and narrow from now on, you understand me?'

Lizzie nodded – because she had to. But she was fighting a dizzy anger inside. Her father was a two-faced bullying liar, and her mother put up with his cruelty to the point where she went to the doctor's and told lies about it. And as her mother got up to sit in the shade of the garden, what did she pick up from the floor? Grandad Powell's walking cane, and limped through the scullery with it.

'Mum! What's the matter with your leg?'

Her mother's wince was a smile gone wrong. 'I dropped the baked bin can on my ankle, lamb. Silly sausage, aren't I?'

Lizzie blew out her cheeks. There was nothing to say to that, no words possible. She wanted to go to the kitchen, open the cupboard, get hold of the other cans and throw them at her father's head. Yes, kill him if she could, twice over. But instead, she gave her arm to her mother and helped her out to the garden and a wicker chair.

'Was Dr Marr kind? Did he charge very much . . .?' The doctor was a pernickety man – had he really believed their lies?

'Don't pester your mother.' There was no chance for an answer. 'She wants a bit of peace and quiet.' Her father had followed them out. 'Start getting the tea. You've got a lot of ground to make up.'

He stayed in the garden dead-heading his roses while Lizzie set a pot of potatoes on the gas ring. She found the sliced ham they'd brought in with them and went down the garden for cabbage, which Jack Parsons cut as if their stalks were necks. It would be a very ordinary tea and he'd either push it away or gobble it down, but Lizzie would bet anything he'd give the Woodman a miss tonight; he'd known since Thursday that there was rebellion in the wind.

But what he didn't know was how strong it would blow. And neither did Lizzie – until she woke up next morning to find her father gone for his Saturday morning shift, and she suddenly found herself taking a wild chance. There'd be just the time if she was quick.

She had the shopping for Sunday in her basket when she ran from the shops up to Rose Cottage and knocked at Joe's door. She was past worrying about his gran, but Joe answered it anyway.

'I took a chance, Joe. You're here.'

'My good luck, then.' He grinned. 'No secret notes to blow away today?'

'Not any more. Everything's out in the open.'

'Well, come and say hello to Gran. She's been fed so she won't bite.' He sounded bouncy and normal.

'Joe, do you know what's been happening with me?' Lizzie thought the whole of Plumstead had to know.

'How would I? You've done some shopping, I can see that.'

The front door opened into the living room where Joe's gran was sitting near a window darning a sock. She showed no surprise at seeing Lizzie. 'Come in, love. No ceremony in this house.' She lifted the sock. 'He knows how to wear a hole, this bloke. It's all that shifting about in his boots . . .'

Lizzie dived straight into things. 'I'm sorry to barge in – but, Joe, I've come to say why I shan't see you on Sunday . . .'

Gran Gibson put down her work basket. 'Assignations. I'll skedaddle out of it.'

'No, please . . .' The old woman seemed very friendly, and there was a softness in her voice that Lizzie liked. Joe dragged a dining chair beneath her and with her head down Lizzie somehow started to speak, with hiccups, and swallows and a glass of water – but eventually out it all came.

'After you saw me in Woolwich . . . I've . . . been in a cell . . . in the police station . . . all one night . . . with the suffragettes . . . and my father's thrown a fit. And he's . . . really hurt my mum this time, enough to go to the doctor's . . . and I'm the cause of it . . .' Her head was in her hands, abject misery.

'Lizzie! Poor Lizzie!' Joe's arm was round her shoulders.

'You poor little love . . .' Gran Gibson came over to put a handkerchief against her forehead.

Lizzie told them everything: why she'd been at the Seamen's Hall, the demonstration, the smoke bomb, her standing up to her father, and her mother ending up at Dr Marr's on account of what he'd done to her. But neither Joe nor his gran asked any questions, they just took what she told them without showing surprise or shock, and gradually Lizzie became more composed. Until the mantelpiece clock chimed half past eleven.

'I've got to go.' Lizzie gripped the table and stood up. 'There'll be murders if I'm not back when he gets in from work.'

Joe was shifting his feet and opening his mouth, but Gran Gibson got in first. 'Well I'll tell you something, girl. And I mean it.' She held Lizzie by both arms. 'Just you let your mother know that we're here, Joe and me. There's refuge for you both at Rose Cottage if ever you need it. Don't think twice about coming up here, promise me.'

'Thank you, Mrs . . .'

'Promise me.'

Lizzie nodded.

'Gran. Call me Gran, lovie.'

'Thank you.'

'But tell your mum nothing much worthwhile was ever won without a fight – and it's surprising what a dose of ginger can do for you.'

Joe picked up Lizzie's basket. 'I'll come with you to The Slade.' He grabbed his cap and opened the front door. 'I won't be long, Gran.'

'Take your time as far as I'm concerned.' Gran leant on the table, a smile on her face. 'Love's young dream never missed me out altogether.'

'Don't take any notice of her – she loves a soppy book.' Joe opened the gate.

Out of the house, it was good to be alone with Joe. Lizzie had been on her own against the world since she'd been put in a cell and separated from Charlotte; now she was with this special boy who seemed to understand her. She sneaked a look at his face as he negotiated a crack in the uneven paving, and she thought how it had all been about *her* these days.

'What was it, Joe – what was it you were going to ask me about? You know, about your work?'

'Oh, that. That's nothing for now. Crikey, you've got enough worms in your can to be going on with.'

'No, go on.' The way things were looking she might not see Joe for a while.

He stopped. 'My job . . .'

'Don't stop. Walk and talk.'

Which was easier said than done for Joe – but he carried on, twisting to her. 'What I'm doing in the Arsenal . . . well, what would you say to helping me with a bit of homework, now and then – when things get settled?'

That was a surprise. 'What sort of homework?'

'School stuff.' He did his best to hurry on. 'I'm thinking of going for an Arsenal Trade Lad, but you have to do an examination.' He took hold of Lizzie's hand. 'It's a dead-end job that I'm doing and I want to get something better. In the Arsenal there's all sorts of different trades, proper trades. What do you think? I fancy going for something, better myself.'

Dear Joe. Of course she'd help him if she could. And he was the sort who needed to get on. He'd left school too early for a bright boy. 'Well I think it's a very good idea. It'll be fun to do together.' And she pictured it: in his kitchen when she could get away, two heads over one book.

But, panic, had she been too caught up in this? Had the Arsenal hooter sounded? Because her father wouldn't hang about coming home today. 'I've got to race now or I'll cop it.' She broke into a little run.

'Yeah, you go.' He gave her the basket and kissed her quickly. 'I'm sorry for everything that's happening.' He kept pace with her for a few yards. 'You look after yourself, Lizzie – and remember what Gran said.' With a faithful salute he stopped running and turned back towards Rose Cottage.

Lizzie hurried for home – with so much going on she was finding it hard to keep things straight. Everything was all jumbled around in her brain and she hardly knew who she was any more. So that when she got to the front door it didn't seem strange that it looked different. Not new paint. Not a new knocker. It just didn't look like the street door of her childhood any more.

Chapter Fourteen

Alice Parsons was disabled all weekend. Lizzie did everything she could to help, the fetching and carrying, the peeling and boiling, the sweeping and scrubbing; and whenever the parlour couch became uncomfortable she helped her mother up the stairs to lie on her bed. This being busy helped, because most jobs around the house meant keeping a close eye on what you were doing – and Lizzie certainly did not want to look at her father. He was already a man with a spiteful secret – but with the secret that had taken her mother to Dr Marr's surgery he had become a stranger she didn't want to know.

There wasn't a breath of air coming through Lizzie's window that Monday morning; it had the feel of thunder and there was dampness in the air as Lizzie made the breakfast – but her mother seemed very calm and cool sitting at the table, giving herself an occasional fan with a place mat. She had a fresh bandage on her arm and was trying to look bright – smiling, even, as if everything in the world was normal.'Thank you, lamb, your eggs are perfectly boiled.'

'More tea?'

'I'll get it.' Alice winced as she twisted to stand up.

'No, me.' But her mother's grateful smile was a pathetic sight.

Her mother started to sing.

'*So here hath been dawning*

Another blue day:

Think, wilt thou let it

Slip useless away?'

She trilled it high as if she were standing joyful in the Mission choir.

Lizzie plonked the teapot on to the draining board. So who was her mother trying to fool? She was a suffering woman twisting about in pain, yet she was putting on this stupid face of happiness. How could she behave like that? What sort of deceiver had she become? Lizzie felt so angry that as soon as she had poured her mother's second cup she went upstairs to get away from the cloying atmosphere in the kitchen. She went to her dressing table drawer and lifted the lining to where the *Votes For Women* newspaper lay hidden. Joan of Arc was still sitting proud on her horse holding her sword aloft – such a different picture of womanhood from Alice Parsons, injured and in pain yet smiling vapidly, a submissive creature to her husband, a domestic slave, the sort of person the women at Catford and Hyde Vale were strong about. And turning through the newspaper, the comparisons between her mother and the women in its pages made the anger inside Lizzie hurt so much that she very nearly threw herself on to her bed to thrash and cry. Hands shaking, she dressed in her school clothes – small buttonholes and fiddly hooks and eyes – and gathered her books and went downstairs, direct to the front door. She'd call goodbye from there and get out of this atmosphere. But her mother came tottering along the hallway carrying her sandwiches. There was never a parting, summer or winter, late or on time, when she didn't see her off to school with a kiss.

'Here you are, lamb. Take your time eating the cheese. Digest it properly, remember, thirty chews for every bite. Your mum knows best.'

Which did it for Lizzie.

She rounded on her, glared at her. 'Knows best? You pathetic person! You're a disgrace to the women of this country!' – words that had been going round in her head.

'*What?*' Her mother reeled, leant against the wall.

'Don't think I don't know what's going on!' She pushed her face into hers. 'I know what he does to you when I'm in bed! I know full well how he hurts you, does things he never should – while you do nothing to stop him. Nothing! And if you're gladly letting him get away with it I'm ashamed of you!'

God! It had come out: the frustration of these months, the pity, and now the anger. She had said it, raised her voice with it, turned her mother's placid face to a twisted, ugly anger. Her mouth was screwed up in a way Lizzie had never seen as she struggled for breath and raised her arm to hit her – but it was her bandaged arm and she could only wince and let out a scream that took a row of pigeons flapping off the rooftop.

'You wicked girl! You stupid, wicked child! How dare you speak to your mother like that! What vile thoughts are in your head? What filth of an imagination's at work in there? Get out! Get out of this house!' Grasping the door's edge she flung it shut with a great slam.

'I will get out! I will! I'm . . . I'm . . .' – and Lizzie finally found the words – 'I'm disgusted to have a mother like you! Disgusted!' She shouted it through the letter box and ran into the street. Her throat thick and tight, she headed towards school, running the length of Plumstead Common Road until her breath had gone and she had to walk up Plum Lane towards Greenfield, her blood pounding less in her head. *And until the thought of what she had done started turning her to ice.* Reality came back. She had lost her senses, gone mad, got carried away and behaved like a little fool. How could she have said those things? What in heaven's name had happened to her? She wasn't Lizzie Parsons any more, she was acting like a Charlotte or a Mrs Crayfourd and got way beyond herself.

She turned around and ran for home. She had never parted from her mother on bad terms. They were friends. In so many day-to-day ways they were allies in her father's household, the two people in the Sutcliffe Road house who should be on the same side – and now they were at odds with each other, massively, like enemies. Disagreements going to school had happened before, of course they had, petty fallings-out over shoes or gloves or the length of her nails; but within minutes she would run back home or her mother would come hurrying to the end of the street, and they'd kiss and make up and Lizzie would let the rest of the day take care of the lump in her throat. Never had a school day gone from morning to home time with bad feeling between them. But today it had happened in a wild temper tantrum that changed everything.

She couldn't get home fast enough. Those words she'd used had been hateful; they froze her in the thundery heat, and she had to beg for forgiveness. She had said to her mother what she should be saying to her sadistic father – but she hadn't had the courage. Oh, what a crass, cowardly, arrogant fool she had become.

'Forgot your drawers, Lizzie Parsons?'

She ignored the rude boy in the street and knocked on her front door. There was no answer. She knocked again, a little harder, but she didn't want to make it sound bad-tempered.

'*Lottie Collins lost her drawers,*

Will you kindly lend her yours . . .?'

'I'll lend you a kick up the backside, Harry Plank!' She looked through the letter box but the kitchen door was shut; all she could see was the empty hallway. She wanted to give the door a bang loud enough to be heard in the scullery but this blessed boy was hanging about having his fun, standing in the road with his hands on his hips. Any other day and she would have roasted him, but she wanted things quiet on her doorstep. She gave one more knock, a lot harder.

'You must be desprat!'

The door still wasn't opened – and Lizzie knew why: not because her mother hadn't heard the knocking but because she wouldn't answer it. She wasn't out; she was too upset after those terrible things said in temper and anger, words that could never be taken back. Now there was a rift between them that might never be healed. She came away. She gripped the straps of her satchel like a slingshot and ran at Harry Plank, who was posturing in the road until she got close, when he ran off blowing raspberries – and she ran off, too, headed for Plum Lane again and school. Oh, dear God, why hadn't she kept her mouth shut? What sort of a disgrace of a daughter was she to have said what she had to a woman who was under the thumb of her husband? Could there ever be forgiveness for what she had done – in this life and the next?

A sultry sun was breaking through as Miss Abrahams found Lizzie in the quadrangle at the end of break and told her to go with her to the Study. There was only one Study and that was Miss Tudor Hart's. Oh, Lord, was there some hangover from the demonstration at the Labour Party, some court business, like a statement the police wanted her to make?

'Come along, chop-chop.'

Lizzie followed Miss Abrahams up to the first floor, nothing said all the way, nor as they waited at the open Study door.

'Come in.'

Miss Tudor Hart was silhouetted against the open window fanning herself with a folder, and thank goodness she was alone. 'I shan't keep you long, Eliza, and don't look so frightened, I'm not going to bite you. On the contrary, Miss Abrahams has something to read to us.' The headmistress waved them both to sit.

Miss Abrahams took a folded piece of paper from

the pocket of her skirt. She opened it and held it up before her like a precious document shown at an auction. 'Dear Miss Tudor Hart (*et cetera, et cetera*) . . .' she read in her Elizabeth Barratt Browning voice, 'The panel of judgment for the League of British Girls' Schools' Trust annual poetry competition has decided that this year's League poetess shall be Greenfield Girls' High School's Eliza Parsons with her poem *Res Et Verba*.' Miss Abrahams's face creased with pride. 'We give her and her school our hearty congratulations. Eliza Parsons will therefore be invited to recite her poem to the Annual General Meeting of the League at the Methodist Central Hall Westminster on 25th July *hoc anno*. The school will also receive the Trust's prize of twenty-five pounds to be used for the purchase of literary works for the school library . . .'

'Thank you, Miss Abrahams.' Miss Tudor Hart held both hands out to Lizzie. 'Eliza, well done, well done indeed! We're both very, very proud of you, aren't we?'

'Enormously proud, Headmistress. I think it's the first time –'

'Excellent, excellent. And from the pen of our Plumstead scholarship girl.' But the smile on Miss Tudor Hart's face had faded. 'Aren't you pleased, Eliza? These things aren't won every day you know.'

Lizzie was still numb. None of this meant anything to her. 'Yes, ma'am, yes I am.' She didn't give tuppence about the poetry prize. 'I'm just surprised. Ever so surprised.'

'Well, then, more of this anon. But time is short. The next thing is the recitation, and we must make it as good as others have ever given. Better.'

The thought appalled Lizzie, standing up in Westminster Central Hall reciting her rubbishy poem. She didn't want to do it, any more than she wanted to stay at this school, or ever go home, or live on this earth. 'It's marvellous!' But she knew her smile would have made a cat sick.

'Then come with me, Eliza.' Miss Abrahams was her matter-of-fact self again. 'I have a break in my timetable and you have PT. I've spoken to the sergeant and absented you. We shall go to my room and rehearse reading the work.'

The work! That took Lizzie by surprise. Miss Abrahams always talked about the 'works' of William Wordsworth and the 'works' of Charles Dickens; now it was the 'work' of Eliza Parsons, and before last Wednesday she'd have been thrilled to hear it. But nothing in her life could ever be thrilling again; it was too dire.

And so the practice recitation suffered.

'Well, I'm surprised, Eliza, and disappointed.' Lizzie had read her poem cold and made a lot of mistakes. And the next reading was no better. 'It's not there yet, Eliza, by a long chalk.' Lizzie sort of tried with the third reading but *Res Et Verba* didn't mean a thing to her; she just wanted to be out of there. 'Lift the voice. Light and shade. You can't mumble like that to a Westminster audience.' Lizzie read it once more but the words went into the floorboards. 'Really, girl! You read so well in class. I think you're not in the mood, not in the mood at all – and I can't imagine why, unless it's your recent escapade.' Miss Abrahams didn't stamp her foot but she creaked a floorboard. 'We'll practise this again tomorrow, but I hope you're not going to fail the school in her moment of glory.'

Lizzie mumbled some sort of apology and was allowed to leave. She dropped down the stairs and headed for the gymnasium, but she didn't get there – she turned off at the last moment, went to the cloakroom for her beret and walked out of the building. Her stupid poem! She would get herself home and hope and pray her mother could find some Christian forgiveness in her heart.

And dear God, she needed it.

Chapter Fifteen

The day had become more humid and Lizzie was uncomfortable hurrying home, in body and mind – and more so when she knocked at the door and got no answer again. The first time it was a 'sorry' knock, the second time a bolder one, and at the last a frustrated bang-bang-bang-bang-bang; but as she peered through the letter box the same empty hallway looked back at her.

Should she knock at Mrs Farmer's next door? But what would she say? Mrs Farmer was a close neighbour and would want to know too much. She looked up and down the street – and there was Mrs Armstrong over the road, coming to her front gate.

'She's gone out, lovie, not fifteen minutes back.'

'Did she say where?'

'Said she's going to see an aunt. It was as if she wasn't with us. Leaning on a stick, she was, not looking to left or to right, limping off and crossing the main road.'

'Not to the shops, then?'

'No, down Lakedale Road. But the funniest thing! On a muggy day like this she's wearing that thick coat of hers, her winter one. I can't keep myself cool as it is . . .' She blew down the top of her blouse in an unladylike way. 'She must be in a proper state . . .'

What? Lizzie was stunned. She got out a thank you and ran for the end of the road. Heaven help her – if her mother had turned down Lakedale Road, Lizzie knew where she was going. To the trams. There was only one aunt near enough to visit, and she lived over the other side of the river. Aunt Elsie. And to get to her they always went on the ferry. *Her mother was heading for the ferry – in a hot coat on a hot day.* Oh, God, was she was going to throw herself under a paddle wheel? Lizzie ran fast for Lakedale Road.

. . . And all because of her! All because she'd lost her temper and said those terrible things. Oh Lord, this was awful! This was the worst thing that could ever have happened – and she had got to stop it!

She had never run so fast – she pelted down the hill to Plumstead High Street and the trams, hot, sticky, and if she hadn't got the fare, ready for a row with the conductor. But there was no one waiting at the tram stop, she'd just missed a tram and it could be a while before the next. So did she wait, or run towards the ferry? It was a good long way. Come on, tram! She wiped her face on her sleeve and was just about to turn and run when she saw one coming – a number 42.

'Woolwich Ferry only. Turning round. Hold tight, please.'

She did find the penny half-fare and sat downstairs, quicker for getting off. But the journey took for ever, along to Woolwich, a hold-up outside the Arsenal main gates, then on towards the ferry, where she got round the back of the conductor and jumped off the tram yards before it stopped.

'Stupid girl!'

She ran for the pier and the ferryboat, just in time, as it was finishing loading. And with no doubt where she was going – straight for the nearest paddle wheel. But, there was no Alice Parsons! She wasn't there – only a couple of boys waiting for the thrashing water. She ran to the other side of the boat but she wasn't there either. She looked into the saloon – but they were all strangers staring back. Where could her mother be? She'd had a quarter of an hour start, but Lizzie had got down Lakedale Road a lot quicker than she could, so this boat would be the one . . .

The hooter sounded, chains clanked, the deck shuddered, the paddle wheels started turning and the boat pulled away from the pier. A deck hand finished coiling a mooring line.

'Excuse me, is everything all right?'

'Why wouldn't it be?'

'There hasn't been any –' What did you say? Accidents? Drownings? Tragedies? The words turned her stomach. 'Nothing's happened, has it?' But what could there have been, the wheels had hardly started turning.

'Stand away, will you, mind that wet line.'

Lizzie went halfway up the steps towards the vehicle deck where there was a better view across the river. If anything had happened on the earlier boat she might see a crowd on the far pier, or a police launch. But everything seemed very normal: a large wagon pulled by two dray-horses was boarding the other vessel over there, the ramp gates closing. If there'd been trouble, the other ferry would have stayed docked, wouldn't it – for the police to investigate. She carried on up to the deck. Ferrymen always shouted at people up here who weren't with the vehicles, so Lizzie kept her head low and edged towards the side of the boat. Had her mother come up here for a better place to jump? She looked along the length of the vessel but there was no sign of her on this side. She scuttled across to the opposite rail, past a motor van and almost burning her hand on a hot radiator. One quick look – but there was still nothing to see, no one.

So had she got this all wrong?

And, *help!* The terrible thought hit her. What if her mother hadn't come to Woolwich at all? The top of Lakedale Road and the top of the ravine steps were practically the same place. What if she'd told Mrs Armstrong a falsehood and gone down the steps to the ravine pond? It was deep enough to drown people, it had happened.

And now there was nothing she could do about it; this ferry had to get to the other side, let its vehicles off, load up and come back again before she could even start to head for home.

And her mother would be dead by then.

She stared at the bridge and started thinking about asking the captain to turn the ferry back – when she suddenly caught sight of something near the deck rail, on the wrong side. Someone. Was it a ferryman? A carter? She bent low to see and hit her head on the metalwork – but then she saw who it was, hidden behind a cartload of barley: her mother, wrapped in her winter coat and sitting on the awning that ran over the walkway of the deck below – and very near to the paddle wheel. Her legs were curled up beneath her the way a child would sit, and ripples off the water reflected the sun on her face giving her a lost and bewildered look. A quick push-off, a short slide across the awning, and her mother would be in the river and under the white spume.

Lizzie shouted at her – but not 'Mum!', not 'Hello': she went straight at her.

'Don't you love me?' she yelled. 'Is this how much you love me?' She'd got to shock her to stop her. She waved at the water. 'Blooming easy for you, isn't it? Bye-bye worries! I'm off, cheerio! But what about your daughter?'

Her mother looked as if she didn't know who she was. Any moment she could be gone.

'*What about Lizzie Parsons?*' Lizzie shrieked it.

Her mother shifted an inch, twisted her head a little, narrowed her eyes – but turned away and sat staring out over the water. No one on the deck was taking any notice, she was behind that barley cart – and if they had, no one could have got to her before she went. Lizzie froze, watching for any movement. Should she say some more? Would *any* words work?

The ferryboat was throbbing, the paddle wheels were turning and frothing, horses were clomping their hooves, a couple of wagoners were cursing one another and a seagull was swooping and screaming – ferry life was going on while no one took a blind bit of notice of a woman who was going to kill herself. Lizzie wanted to move closer to her but she daren't; she mustn't panic her mother before she could get near enough to stop a sudden push and slide.

So she stood up and thumped her chest bone.

'What about me, Alice Parsons? Would you leave me alone with him? Seventeen years of you giving me all that love, then one falling out and you're saying goodbye for ever! Huh!'

But now her mother had turned her gaze to the paddle wheel going round and round, its drips catching the sun, and she seemed to be hypnotised by it, and after several revolutions she lifted her eyes to Lizzie and began to speak – in a voice so clear and firm she might have been giving testimony at the Mission.

'You told me what you thought of me this morning, didn't you, Lizzie? Well it's true. Yes, it's true.' She nodded as if to confirm it in her own mind. 'I'm a disgraced and shamed woman, just as you said I was.' She looked away to squint at the sky, came back. 'And how much worse can a woman be? And what can be worse for a mother than to be despised by her daughter?' She looked at the water, looked back at Lizzie. 'Well, now I've lost mine and there's no one to live for any more.' It was as if she were pronouncing a sentence on herself. She shifted again and looked again at the water – sharply, as if she might suddenly carry it out.

But Lizzie didn't plead. Persuasion would be weak and useless right now.

'Oh, what a silly old fool you look!' Surprise was better. 'Sitting there on the hottest day of the year wearing that woollen winter coat like some down-and-out from Ropeyard Rails. I suppose you think it'll take you under the water like that woman in your story.' She bent closer to make her point. 'But wool's got all those curly air pockets, hasn't it? It's not like fur or leather. Have you ever seen a drowned sheep?' Lizzie hadn't either but it was something to say. 'They float like boats for miles . . .'

Her mother pulled at the coat's sleeve to look at it, so Lizzie went on talking, changing her tone. She crouched as close as she dared. 'Listen. You have *not* lost me, Mum, and you never will. You are the most precious person in my world and I love you more than you could ever think. You're my dear mother, my dear, dear Mum. Your love is the best thing anyone could ever have. Are you going to take that away from me? Are you going to rob me of my mother? And what about you?' Lizzie went on, her eyes filling with tears, 'Does anyone deserve to treat themselves this badly? And you of all people? Don't you know what a very special person you are – at the Mission, along our street, to the people all over the place who read the letters you write for others?' She had gone on and was running out of things to say, but her mother did seem to be listening: she was pursing her lips the way she did when taking neighbours' instructions. 'Every woman is special, and Alice Parsons is extra-special. You go and kill her and that spiteful man has won, hasn't he? He really will have done his worst to you.'

Lord, had she gone too far? But she wasn't negotiating any more, she was speaking from the heart; there was no other way than this, whatever came of it. 'Listen, we've got a future together, you and me – Alice and Lizzie Parsons – we've got to believe that. You and I are special to each other and we are special to God. So do you want to kill off one of His special creations – because if you do you'll be killing off another one, too.'

Alice was sobbing now. Her head was bent, her shoulders had dropped, and after a huge snatch of breath she had started staring intently at her boots; while with a cautious hand out to her, Lizzie crouched and waited.

Several times her mother looked ready to speak, opened her mouth but closed it again. Then, just as Lizzie was thinking of what more to say to keep some hope alive, her mother's head turned to her and she spoke in a quiet, firm voice.

'Your father was once the big Plumstead prize, Lizzie, the handsomest man at the social dances – and I won him! Miss Alice Freeman from Miriam Road won the man that half Woolwich wanted. Being seen on his arm was to be walking in dreamland. And years later when he won his bravery medal and his picture was printed in the *Kentish,* he was fêted as he declared a new floor open at Cuffs of Woolwich. I was his wife and people tipped their hats to us . . .'

The ferry was in mid-stream, still a fair way from the north pier. Alice straightened her back and her voice became louder.

'. . . I was determined to hold on to him any way I could.' She looked at the sky again, at the river and at the further bank. 'But I paid for the privilege of winning him, Lizzie, and keeping him, and I'm still paying for it . . .'

What could Lizzie say to that? There was only one thing, really. Leaning a little closer she asked the crucial question, the only one that mattered.

'He was a prize and you won it. *But do you love him, Mum? Do you still love him?*' Or was that too incredulous to even ask?

Alice turned and slowly shook her head. 'You don't know what love is, lamb.'

Lizzie didn't answer quickly. Then, 'Perhaps I don't, Mum, but I'm beginning to find out.' Which was the truth. But, lamb! She'd called her lamb. And was she fidgeting away from the edge of the awning, just a little? She was looking at the hem of her coat and back again. Now Lizzie found a different voice from somewhere, maybe a touch of Charlotte's tone, personal but precise. 'Well, love Dad or hate him, you can't go back to him the way things are; we both know that. You won't fool Dr Marr another time – and I won't be fooled either. Nothing's ever going to be the same again.'

Things had to be faced, but was this the time to face them? Alice Parsons wasn't safe until she was this side of the safety rail, and she still looked uncertain, she still needed more reassurance if she was to be persuaded not to jump.

'And let me tell you this, Mum, because it's important.' Lizzie cleared her throat. 'You won't be left on the street, even if he throws you out. There are friends of mine who will take us in.' Perhaps she shouldn't have said it but who cared – her mother needed to know there was an alternative to living in a house with a spiteful husband. And here came the important bit. 'But, Mum, it's not your will that's got to come out on top . . .'

Alice looked at her as if to say, 'What do you mean?'

'. . . It's not his will, either – it's *both* your wills. You could go, of course, and be yourself. But why should you? Dad just can't carry on behaving the way he has been, and if he doesn't agree to changing, then it's him who goes not you. Everything must be different from now on – and it can be, because I'll help it to happen.'

Lizzie had said things today she would never have dreamed of saying. The world had become a different place and she was a different person. Everything from now on would happen in new circumstances – but would they be happening to a mother's daughter . . . or to a grieving girl? What was her mother doing now, drawing up her legs? Was she turning back from the edge – or standing up to jump? Lizzie couldn't physically stop her in time, whichever way it was, so it had to be words, stirring words.

'And your will has got to be a woman's with her own rights. A proud woman's. With my will, and with other women's, standing up for right and justice. Alice Freeman from Miriam Road deserves to live her life in her own right, the same as all her sisters.' Lizzie waved her hand to include all the women of Woolwich, on both sides of the river. 'Alice Freeman? Alice Free-woman!'

Her mother was shifting, leaning on her good arm as if about to take her weight on it.

'It's got to work, Mum. With firm love, on your terms. On women's terms – because I'm going to be in this as well. We stay in the house and we stand up to him and we make things right for all three of us . . .'

The ferry was drawing close to the North Woolwich bank where the currents were wicked and well known. Coat or no coat, no one could survive in their strong swirl. Still out of Lizzie's reach Alice pulled herself up and held on to the rail behind her . . .

'Mum! Mother . . .!' She was going to do something! But she was slipping her arms out of her coat. What trick was this? And her mother threw the coat at her. 'Catch!' she called.

Lizzie caught it and, still wary of any sudden movement, murmuring, 'Mum, Mum, dear Mum . . .' she slowly moved close enough to take her mother's arm. She raised her eyes to the sky. *She wasn't going to jump! She was safe.* Alice picked up the cane that was lying by her side and allowed Lizzie to help her back to the safe side of the rail, and to lead her carefully through the horses and wagons down to the saloon, their talk only of where to hold on, how not to bump their heads or bang their elbows. And once inside the saloon they sat defiant of deck hands while the ferryboat turned around; and stayed hugging each other as it took them back to Woolwich – saying nothing more because there was far too much to say.

Chapter Sixteen

Sutcliffe Road was hot. On Mrs Armstrong's side of the street people were sitting inside shady porches as Lizzie and her mother slipped quietly into the house. They found their own shade in the garden, and with Alice in the wicker chair and Lizzie on a kitchen stool a very difficult conversation began.

'Mum, do you remember reading about that dumb girl in the *Daily Mirror* who was helped to talk again?'

'I do. But . . .' Alice looked puzzled.

'Well, the thing about it was, the paper said she was helped by a . . . a . . .'

'A psychiatrist. Or was it psychologist? I always mix them up. But, what's that got to do with . . .?'

'Psychiatrist, I think. Well, they made a lot about that – but did you know psychiatrists can help with all sorts of other problems? Like, personal things between people . . .' This was not going to be easy.

'Of course.' Her mother had twigged now; she knew what Lizzie was talking about – and she was still frowning. So Lizzie pushed on – this had got to be said. 'Well, a psychiatrist friend of Miss Mitchell's runs a clinic at St Thomas's Hospital, to help people with certain sorts of problems . . .'

The frown became a stare. '*Miss Mitchell*?'

'She's a kind person, Mum, and she understands . . .'

Alice looked horrified. 'You told a teacher about things?'

'Only to help you. I couldn't lie in bed all those nights knowing things were going on and not try to help you, could I?' She leant over and kissed her mother on the cheek. She didn't want to go over their terrible row again.

'Oh, my Lord! The world and his wife knows . . .!'

'No, just two people who want to help: her and me. She says this doctor at St Thomas's sees men like Dad and helps them with their problems.' And Lizzie went on, her mother sitting stony-faced as she told her what Charlotte had said about psychiatry, but she kept things unthreatening: she made no mention of mental illness and she avoided that dreadful word *sadism*; instead, she used words like 'clinic' and 'patient' so as make an appointment at St Thomas's sound like any visit to the doctor's. 'It's something hopeful to offer to Dad,' she ended. 'To put in the pot.'

'It was only ever the arms, my foot was a true accident.' Alice was looking very unhappy now, and Lizzie knew she'd let this out too quickly, but how else to do it? Time was short: her father would be getting in from work very soon.

Alice must have realised this, too, because with a huge huff she changed the subject. 'Well, that's for then, and this is now, Lizzie. He won't be long. How we can all get along in the house, that's what's important today. And we've got to talk it out as soon as he gets in, else we'll lose our will and be back where we started.'

Lizzie leant towards her. 'We'll do it, Mum,' she said.

'He'll be surprised, which will help; and after that we'll have to see which way the cat jumps.' And Lizzie dearly wished it were a cat and not her father who'd be doing the jumping. 'But we must really sit him up, make him take notice, concentrate his mind, be sure he fully understands the ins and outs of us living together . . .'

'And I've got an idea about that – a surprise way to make him listen.' Which she had. It had started forming in her mind as they'd ridden the tram back from the ferry. 'My poem,' Lizzie said. 'We'll start with my poem –' She jumped up and went to the back door. 'I'll get it, and then make a couple of alterations.'

'Alter it? Are you sure?'

'No.' Lizzie was honest. 'More like cut it down, make it a way to start.'

When she came back with her exercise book she sat and wrote – although she was so scared by the thought of what her father might do that when she put pencil to paper her eyes wouldn't focus, and the words danced like goblins. Had she got the nerve to read this to him? Well, she'd soon find out. Meanwhile she worked on, crossing out, putting in, until finally she closed her exercise book and stared at the ground.

'Read it to me. Let me see. Tell me how it's going to sit him up.'

But Lizzie wouldn't. 'It'll work best if you don't know.'

'Oh? Really?' Alice didn't seem too happy over that. But Lizzie tore a sheet from her book and wrote out her new words; and when she'd done that she primed her mother on how they should begin, a sort of introduction she could make, as if they were at the Central Hall, Westminster. By now the air was too heavy for much talk, and they sat and waited, listened to a blackbird singing its territory – until suddenly a door slammed inside the house, Lizzie nearly fell off her stool, and her father came into the garden.

Oh, Lord, could she do it? Did she dare?

Jack Parsons stood and grunted at them, wiping his face with his pocket rag. With her head lowered, Lizzie looked up at him, at those slits of eyes, at his big hands and scarred arms.

'I'll make you a cup of tea, Jack. Then there's something Lizzie wants to do for you.' Somehow Alice's voice sounded normal.

'Before my meal?' he growled.

'It might not take long. But she'd best do it inside . . .'

Lizzie got the sort of look she would expect today. 'Only after I've got out of this shirt.' Jack Parsons went into the house, jabbing a finger back at Alice. 'And you can get me an arrowroot biscuit.'

Typical! But that attitude helped Lizzie. It was a reminder of the sort of man he was – and why she and her mother were doing this. He hadn't even thought to ask how she was, her arm still bandaged up on this hot, mucky day. Lizzie got up from her stool to follow her father indoors, holding her head high in the hope it would make her brave, but she was so scared she could scarcely put one foot in front of the other . . . Because the ten minutes to come were going to change her life, forever.

Alice sat Jack in his favourite chair in the kitchen, told Lizzie to stand by her side, and leaning on the table like a chairwoman at a public meeting she cleared her throat and made her introduction.

'As you know, Jack, the time is getting close for Lizzie to recite her poem at the Westminster Central Hall . . .'

'If I let her,' Jack Parsons growled.

Alice ignored that and went on in a more formal voice, '. . . The poem you're about to hear will be performed before trustees and headmistresses of over thirty schools in the League of British Girls' Schools, and it will be recited not only to them but to the Bishop of London and will be reported upon by *The Times* and the *Daily Mail*, the *Kentish Independent*, and the *Blackheath Gazette*.' She rapped a spoon upon the table as if calling for attention and lifted her hand towards Lizzie. 'Eliza Parsons . . .' she announced. It was just as if they were there already.

'Get on with it.' Jack Parsons dipped his biscuit in his tea, splayed his legs and sat back in his chair, his eyebrows low and his watch chain stretched.

And now was the moment. Lizzie's legs were as weak as reeds and she thought she'd crumple to the floor, but she gripped the back of a kitchen chair and kept herself upright.

'Before the poem begins I shall say what Miss Abrahams has told me to say by way of introduction.' It amazed her that her voice should sound so normal, because her throat felt strangled. She took her folded piece of paper from the pocket of her dress. 'Of course, I shall learn everything by heart before the day.' She steadied herself and deliberately addressed the door to the passage, gazed above her father's head – his expression was one she did not want to see.

'*My name is Eliza Parsons*,' she read, '*a pupil at Greenfield High School for Girls. I live in Sutcliffe Road, Plumstead, with my father John Parsons, who is a superintendent in the Woolwich Arsenal and who holds the Edward Medal for Bravery, and with my mother, who is unfortunately injured at the moment . . .*'

'No need for that.' Jack Parsons sounded like a dog about to bite. 'Your mother will be right as rain.'

'And so to my poem.' Lizzie took a step sideways to stand fully behind the kitchen chair. She filled her lungs as best she could, put a hand to her breast as if to hold her heart in place, and balanced her feet to keep herself standing. Now she paused for a second or two, willing herself into being someone else, someone who wouldn't be petrified at saying what she was about to say. Not Lizzie Parsons but Charlotte Mitchell. And she wasn't in this kitchen; she was in Woolwich Police Station standing before a bullying constable. She cleared her throat – and read her words directly at her father.

'*My father hurts my mum some nights and it often makes her bleed. She covers it up and keeps it quiet in case she's not believed . . .*'

'*Christ!*' Her father's eyes were spot-welded on to his face. He jumped from his chair. 'What the flaming hell . . .?'

'Mind your mouth, Jack!' Alice's voice cut the air sharply. 'And sit down! Lizzie hasn't finished yet.' She, too, was like another person – or someone she might have been – enough for Jack Parsons to slowly sit again, glowering.

Somehow Lizzie held on to being Charlotte.

'*. . . He's supposed to be a hero but he isn't one to me. He's a bigot and a bully and we both want to be free.*'

She got no further. He was up again, fists like rocks. 'You little witch!' He grabbed at the table between him and Alice. 'And as for you . . .'

But adrenaline had taken over, giving force and strength and rightness to Lizzie. She pushed forward between her father and the table – not his daughter but a suffragette fighter facing up to a prison doctor. 'Sit down, Father!' She glared at him. *God! Was he going to hit her?* But she would take it, she would take it. 'The only reason I would *not* read that out at the Westminster Central Hall would be if I were dead, and all Plumstead would know about it. What you've been doing to Mum is no secret any more.' His face was a violent mask, but she didn't give an inch. 'People wouldn't tip their hats to you, they'd spit on the pavement. So all that sadistic business has got to stop.' She pointed at him. 'You leave Mum alone or you'll get your Edward Medal ripped off your chest by the king himself.'

He stared at her, rage and total disbelief on his face,

one fist balled in the palm of the other. 'You wicked little vixen!' He raised his fist high.

And she stood there.

'Jack! Jack! You dare!'

Lizzie suddenly thrust her arms out before her, palms down, level and unshaking. Jack Parsons stared at them, lowering his fist. With her right hand Lizzie slowly rolled up her left sleeve, roll by roll, keeping the arm held out at him, white and unblemished. His eyes were fixed upon it.

'What would a man like you want to do to an arm this? Bite it, cut it, twist it till it tears like paper . . .?'

'*Good God alive!*' He swayed, swore violently.

Her mother was crying, 'Lizzie! Lizzie!'

Would he grab the arm and show her what he'd do to it? For a moment he looked as if he might. But Lizzie kept her voice as steady as her arm. 'Mum's written down what happens in this house and she's left a sealed envelope with the pastor.' Which wasn't true, but she stared him out as if it were. 'So if anything happens to either of us the whole of Plumstead will know about you and your sadism as if it was printed in the *Kentish*.'

'*Jesus Christ!*'

Lizzie blinked at the force of his voice.

'And you can keep Our Lord out of it!' Alice pushed a chair aside. 'Listen to me, Jack, I've been to hell and back. My shame and degradation is . . . bottomless . . .'

She lifted her chin, held her bad arm up at him. 'And, Jack. This stops!' He opened his mouth but she put up a flat palm. The bravery in the room was worth ten Edward medals. 'Hear me out – I said "to hell *and back*".' He was standing differently now, unbalanced. 'And from the depths of where I was, from the hell I was in, our daughter has saved me from killing myself – yes, from killing myself today – and she has brought me home.'

He stared at her, stared and stared – then bent forward at the waist and roared at her like an animal, roared until he was roared out and the sound became the whine of a wounded animal. He straightened up and turned to grab at the door to the passage.

'Please, dear Jack, understand. You know what's right and wrong and you know it had to come to this. You know there had to be an end to it.'

He looked as if he didn't know any such thing.

'So, yes, go out and think things over. Think about you, and me, and Lizzie. Think about our home together. But please don't feel responsible for us. We won't want. I can stand behind a counter at Cuffs of Woolwich as well as any woman. We won't be out on the street.' Then she smiled at him, a smile that started with her mouth and slowly filled her face with tenderness, with love. 'But we'd rather be here with you, Jack, in our home, only with a different order of things.' He let go the door handle then grabbed it again. 'You and I will talk, Jack, on our own, there's so very much to say. And there's hope. And practicality – because together we can get help, both of us, if you'll come with me. Professional help.'

Lizzie stood there, no longer the centre of things, wishing – and not in a cowardly way – that she could quietly disappear. But her mother had come to stand next to her and there was no barrier now between any of them.

'We are the Parsons of Plumstead –' Alice held a hand out to Jack – 'the three of us, our family; and if we want to, we can share this house in love and light and fairness. There's a place in my heart for you, if you can find it.'

He straightened up, said nothing, walked into the passage and returned with his cap on his head.

'We need you, Jack. Do come back to us. We can go together to Westminster when Lizzie reads her poem, the proper poem next time, and together we can be proud of bringing up such an individual daughter.'

Lizzie shifted her feet. Individual meant being different; although in what way she really couldn't tell. But she did *feel* different, and she was proud to hear her mother say it.

Her father was saying nothing, he looked incapable of even trying, and within half a minute he was out of the house.

Lizzie and her mother stood and stared at each other. Lizzie's mind was whirling with all the anger, the fear, the courage and the relief that had taken her over today. And now there was uncertainty. It must have been on her face.

'Rest assured, lamb, when he comes back and, despite appearances, I truly think he will, he'll come back a different man from the man who's just gone out. If I could say nothing else about him I'd say he's a man who recognises what's what.'

'We'll see, Mum dear, we'll see . . .' She felt her mother's cheek against her own.

'Oh, I've been weak, Lizzie, I've been stupid, I can't begin to explain how people like me will behave sometimes; how very weird and surrendering love can be. His poor scarred and burnt arms . . .' She closed her mouth on that. Then, 'But, thank you, lamb – or should I say lion?' Her voice rose and she turned to face Lizzie. She took both her hands in her own. 'Your bravery and your words have made all the difference in the world. Having the courage to speak the truth of things will bring a new beginning, I'm sure of it. What is it your women say, your suffragette motto . . .?'

'*Res Non Verba*. Deeds Not Words.'

Alice repeated it. 'Well I think it should be Deeds *And* Words. They really can't be separated, not in my book – because the deed can sometimes be the courage to speak the words, can't it?'

'*I* think so, Mum – and just you wait until Westminster . . .'

'Westminster? Why, dear?'

'Oh, you'll see.' Lizzie smiled, looked at her mother and kissed her, and thought how much she loved her. And with a warm feeling deep inside her she also thought of two other people she knew, each of them different and courageous, who would always have special places in her heart.

And when she was alone in her bedroom she would blow a kiss to each – to Joe Gibson and to Charlotte Mitchell.

Res et Verba

Eliza Parsons's poem recited by her to the Annual General Meeting of the League of British Girls' Schools at the Methodist Central Hall Westminster on 25th day of July 1912 in the presence of her mother and, separately, her father.

It's not about them, it's more about us,
All the young eyes reading.
It's us who count, not 'the national mood'
Or what they call 'the country'.

The cheering crowd, the common cause,
Those throngs of dedication
For freedom and justice and the righting of wrongs
Are grand ideas but distant.

They're disputed on high in the halls of state,
Among frockcoats and top hats;
Written in papers and speeches and books
That won't make a ha'porth of difference.

Connivance and custom mean London rules
Our suburban scullery.
Apron strings will still be the chains
That show men's domination.

So hear us girls as we learn and grow
To play our proper part.
Our schools will know where we should go
To make a telling start –

To the highest places to rap the doors
Of opportunity –
Not with cudgels but using the power of words.
To gain rightful victory.

An argument fought with sword and gun,
Muscular weaponry,
Can never make hearts and minds improve
The lot of us who come on after.

But words – ideas and truths – can change
Popular opinion;
Bringing ages and sexes side by side
In factory, school and home

Res Et Verba – Deeds and Words.

Winning arguments: To influence both
our leaders and led, and bring hope
to my generation.